THE CONNOLLYS

Cover design by Emma Woodger

THE CONNOLLYS

comprising

Connolly's Pass

and

The Connolly Connection

Jessie Woodger

THE CONNOLLYS
First published as a single volume in 2005

Typeset and published by John Owen Smith
19 Kay Crescent, Headley Down, Hampshire GU35 8AH

Tel: 01428 712892
wordsmith@johnowensmith.co.uk
www.johnowensmith.co.uk

ISBN 978-1-873855-46-1

Printed by CreateSpace

Connolly's Pass

Chapter 1

The big farm kitchen seemed to be empty. The only noise was the loud tick-tock of the ancient clock on the mantelpiece. There it sat, its wood casing darkened by years of peat smoke, pipe smoke and wear and tear, but the brass pendulum still swung steadily, wound up every Sunday morning. A small sniffle broke the silence, and at the little table by the side window a young girl sat over her homework.

Maths were the plague of her life. She could write neatly, and she loved history, grammar and geography—although the lines of latitude and longitude were still a mystery—but try as she would, and she really tried, she went blank on maths. Her teacher, Matthew Webb, had a lot of patience. He found all her other work very good, and had told her so, but here she was trying to master factors, and she didn't have a clue.

The back door opened and her mother came in. 'Liz,' she said, 'put the books away for now and lay up the table. The men will be in soon, starving as usual.' 'Do you know anything about fractions, Mam?' Liz asked. 'No, dear,' was the reply. 'I learned to read and write, add and subtract, and that was all a girl needed to know when I was your age.'

Half an hour later Bob West came in followed by Hughie Connolly and Hughie's son Sean. They all sat round the table. Sean looked at Liz and noticing her eyes still slightly swollen from crying over her homework thought, 'She is still in the dark with the maths.' After they finished eating he went over to the little table. He picked up her book and said, 'What can't you do, Liz?' She came over and they both sat down. He was explaining it to her when her mother, Barbara, said, 'I don't think you should do them for her, Sean.' 'I'm not doing them for her,' he answered. 'I'm showing her how I do them. If she does them for herself on spare paper, I will see if they are right. Then she can write them neatly into her book.' 'How come you are so good at the books, Sean?' Bob West asked. 'I don't know,' Sean replied. 'I liked school, but Dennis is the brains in our family. He is going to be a priest.' 'They are all good at school,' said Hughie, proudly. 'I don't know where they get it from. Rosie, the wife, is a great one with the money. She would know if a halfpenny was missing. All I have to do is bring it home.' They all laughed, and the men went back to the fields.

Hughie and Rosie Connolly had six children. They owned their little cottage with two fields, they had a good vegetable garden and plenty of potatoes. Four goats grazed on what was left, with a few geese, chickens, and ducks. The cottage stood on a hill. To reach the road into the town of Cavan they had to go down the hill and over a bog Pass. The bog was dangerous, with holes filled with water where the peat had been dug out for generations, and no fence on either side. Rosie warned the children every day not to play about on the Pass in case they fell down a hole and disappeared. Even so, she stood half way down the hill when they went to school and again when they came home. She had nightmares about the bog. It looked so pretty in spring, covered with heather in bloom, but Rosie knew how much danger lay underneath.

For generations the Connollys had worked for the Wests. Bob West was a well-to-do farmer, working a hundred acres. His son, Robert, was at Trinity College reading medicine. Bob wondered who would run the farm when he died. He hoped Liz would marry a farmer and take it on. Robert helped out when he was at home but showed no interest in the running of it, although having a son who was a doctor was a fine thing. Bob and Barbara had had another son, two years younger than Liz, but he had died in infancy. Barbara was forty-two when he was born and no more children had come along.

One evening in late October, Hughie and Sean came in from work. It was Saturday and Rosie had been ironing all afternoon, clothes for Mass in the morning for all of them. Hughie put his arm round her waist and said, 'How are we off for money? I fancy a Guinness.' Rosie went to the old china teapot and took out a ten shilling note. 'Can we spare it?' he asked. 'You can have a drink my love,' she said, 'you don't go out very often.' 'That's a fact,' he said, 'I can't remember when I last went out with John, Pat and Jack. I'll be back by ten o'clock.' The four men had grown up together, went to school, and had married the same year.

Hughie washed, shaved, changed and left the house. Rosie bathed the children and gave them their supper. Patsy, the youngest, she put to bed and the next three, all girls, wanted to play ludo for a while. Sean and Dennis sat by the fire, reading. Rosie tidied the room, then went out, shut the chicken house, and closed in the ducks and geese. She looked down the hill. There was a faint mist over the bog. She felt restless. She went back indoors. Sean looked up. 'What's wrong, Mam? Can't you sit down and have a warm?' He pushed her chair closer to the big peat fire. 'I feel uneasy,' she said. 'I'll make us a cup of tea,' Dennis said. She sat and drank the tea and then started walking round the room again. Her sons watched her. She was usually glad to sit down in the evening, having worked hard all day.

At nine o'clock Sean and Dennis went to bed. Rosie sat at last and dozed. Suddenly she woke, and jumped up. She looked at the clock. It was almost midnight. Where was Hughie? He was always home by ten. She went out. The fog was thick now. She felt that something had woken her. She checked the children, all sleeping. Little Patsy sucked his thumb, his cheeks rosy and his curls spread out on the pillows. She went back to the living room, made up the fire and sat and waited. As time passed she grew more worried. She thought of waking Sean, but she was afraid he would rush out and get lost in the fog. At six o'clock she finally called him. 'Sean, son, wake up! Your father hasn't come home and I'm worried about him.' Sean blinked and rubbed his eyes. 'What time is it?' he asked. 'It's turned six o'clock. I don't know what to do,' she replied. Sean dressed and drank the tea she poured for him. 'I'll go and look for him,' he said. 'Don't go down the Pass,' she said. 'Go across the back field and down into West's back meadow. The fog is thick out there.'

Sean ran across the field, jumped the fence and ran down the meadow. When he reached West's house he saw a light in the kitchen. He knocked the back door and Bob West opened it. Sean was panting and crying. 'Mr West, me Da went for a drink last night and he hasn't come home. Ma is off her head with worry and she hasn't been to bed.' 'Come in, Sean. Sit down.' He pulled a chair out, and Sean sat. 'Now, who was he drinking with, and where did they go?' 'He always goes with John and Pat Donaghue and Jack McKenna, and they walk down to Kelly's. He never drinks much, and he's always home by ten.' Bob West went to tell his wife, then he and Sean got into his car and drove to John Donaghue's.

The Donaghues were still in bed, but John came to the door. He told them the pub was very quiet, they had each bought a round of drinks, half pints of Guinness, and had left at about half past nine. Hughie wasn't drunk, none of them were, and they had parted at the crossroads. 'I called to him, "Don't get lost in the fog", and he shouted back, "I could get home blindfolded".'

Bob had decided to go to the Gardai, but he dropped Sean off and asked Barbara to go and see Rosie.

The Gardai searched for four hours. The fog didn't lift until two o'clock. Then one of the Gardai saw a check flat cap stuck in the weeds at the side. Poor Hughie's bloated body was dredged up at four. The Gardai took him away. There would have to be an inquest, they told Rosie gently. Even the toughest one of them had found it hard to tell her that she was a widow, with five children to fend for. The neighbourhood was in shock. The bog had been there a long time, but this was its first victim. A young man of forty, strong and fit. It was a tragedy.

Barbara West and Liz hurried through the milking, fed the livestock and went over the meadow to Connolly's. Sean was standing outside, his eyes dull and his shoulders sagging. Barbara put her arms around him and held him; he was in shock. Rosie sat with little Patsy on her knee, her face swollen with crying. The little girls sat on the settee bed in a stiff little row, wondering what was going on. Bob West had taken Dennis with him to tell both Rosie and Hughie's relatives. Barbara asked Liz to take the three little girls home and look after them and give them some food. Liz asked if she should take little Patsy as well, but Barbara said she thought that Patsy was good for Rosie, so Liz took the girls home and fed them and read them a story. Afterwards, the smallest one, Nuala, asked, 'Has daddy gone to heaven?' Liz cuddled her and said, 'Yes.' 'When will he be back?' Nuala asked. Poor Liz, only thirteen years old, didn't know how to answer her. The eldest, Maura, said, 'He's dead, he won't be back.' Kathleen and Nuala started crying. Liz was at her wits' end when the back door opened and Bob came in. He saw Liz was distressed and said, 'Who would like a ride in my car?' They all wiped their eyes and he drove them to the sweet shop, where he bought them all a bar of chocolate and one to take home for Patsy. When they got home, three of Rosie's sisters had arrived with Hughie's sister and her husband. Barbara, Liz and Bob left the family to their grief.

'What will become of Rosie with all those children?' Barbara asked worriedly. 'She is such a good woman. She's a wonderful mother, she doesn't deserve this at all.' Bob put his arm around her. 'Things will sort themselves out—and we won't let them go hungry.'

The inquest was the following day. 'Death by Misadventure' was the coroner's verdict and no one could argue with that. The funeral was the next day, as is the custom in Ireland; two nights' wakes and burial on the third day. The neighbouring women all bring food, cakes, scones, sandwiches, tea, milk, sugar, and everyone at the funeral goes back to the house. To some, that seems like hard work. But family and friends all gathered together strengthens the bereaved. After everyone had gone, Rosie found enough food in the house to feed her family for a week. Surrounded by her friends, she still had time to think and was convinced that she should move away. She couldn't bear to look down the bog Pass for the rest of her life. When Bob and Barbara came late in the evening, she told them she would have to leave. She didn't know when, but the sooner the better.

Bob's brother-in-law had opened a small shoe factory in Belturbet and Bob called in to see whether he could help. He said he needed a couple more people. Bob then started to look for a small vacant house. He called at the bank and had a cup of coffee with the manager, an old friend, and asked if he knew where he could find one. He told him the whole sad story, which the manager had heard about although he didn't know that Rosie wanted to move. 'That will be two workers short at your place,' he said. 'I know,' sighed Bob. 'Hughie was a great worker, and young Sean is too, but Rosie is going to make herself ill if she stays there. She hasn't walked on that Pass since Saturday, and she won't let the children walk on it either.' The manager was silent for a few minutes, then he said, 'There is a cottage out the Cavan Road. Old Tod Butler was ill all winter and has gone to live with his daughter. The son-in- law works here in the bank. I will find out if Rosie could have it. Call in tomorrow and we will see.'

When Bob called at the bank the next day, Old Tod and his daughter were there. Tod looked frail. He agreed to rent the cottage to Rosie and her family. He remembered Hughie and felt sorry for them. Bob went home and talked to Rosie and the family, telling them that Sean and Dennis could work in the factory. He didn't know what they would be doing, but he would take them to the factory to talk to the boss. Rosie listened, and when he had finished she said, 'Sean would be glad of the work, but Dennis has to continue at school.   Hughie had set his heart on Dennis studying for the priesthood and that is it.' 'How are you going to manage for money?' Bob asked. 'I can rent the two fields out. I will have to sell the goats, but there is a bit of garden around the cottage so I'll keep the chickens and ducks. The geese will have to go too, but somehow we will manage.' So at the end of the week Rosie, her children and her belongings moved to the cottage on the Cavan Road. It was about the same size as the house she had left.

Sean had been to the factory and was offered a job in the store. Bob had told the boss, Mr Wilson, that Sean was good and bright, so he was shown how to book in the deliveries and, as each department put in requisition notes, how to check everything coming in and going out and list all the orders, and how to re-order stock. It was a lot of responsibility for a lad of eighteen, but the pay was better than Hughie's had been and, provided that Sean was willing to be the breadwinner, for the time being Rosie felt she could manage.

After his first week, Mr Wilson mentioned that he needed an evening cleaner to tidy the place when the workers had gone home, two hours on six days each week. Sean told Rosie, who talked to the children. They promised to look after Patsy for a couple of hours each day. It was one shilling per hour, but it would pay the rent and leave a bit to put aside for when Dennis started college.

Liz West missed the Connollys. She had had great affection for Hughie. He had been around all her life, he had carried her through the fields, showed her the robin's nest in the old peat shed and lifted her high above his head to peep into the blackbird's nest in the lane. Sean was a special friend too, so clever. It was like losing part of her family. She wandered up to the bog Pass and came to the place where Hughie had been found. It was all trampled and untidy, so she went into the woods and dug up some wild primroses and bluebell bulbs. When she brought them back, she planted them on the edge of the bog hole.

'Where have you been?' Barbara asked. 'And look at your hands.' 'I was looking for mushrooms,' Liz said. 'At this time of year! Honestly, Liz, I don't know what is going to become of you. Wash your hands and change those shoes, your tea is in the oven.'

In bed later, Barbara told Bob, but he said, 'She's missing the Connollys. You know how Hughie spoiled her, and Sean was a close friend. Girls of her age feel things for a while. She'll recover when Robert comes home for Christmas. I'll have to look for a couple of workers soon as there's a lot of fencing to do. I won't find one like

Hughie. I'll have to keep an eye on things for a while. It's the hiring fair in Cavan this Tuesday. I'll see if I can find a couple.' 'Where are they going to sleep?' Barbara asked. 'I don't want workmen sleeping in the house.' 'I've been thinking about that,' he replied. 'Perhaps Rosie would rent them the cottage. It would be a pity to let it fall down, and she might be glad of a few shillings rent. I must go and see her, see if she needs anything. I will say this for her, she's a survivor. But she must be going through hell without Hughie.' 'I will bake a cake and send her some eggs and butter and a can of milk,' Barbara said.

Bob went to the hiring fair and brought back a father and son, Peter Kennedy and his son Paul. They had been recommended by a friend, both good workers. Barbara didn't really like them. She thought their speech was rough, and they looked like a couple of prizefighters. She told them she would cook them a midday meal but they would have to have their breakfast and evening meal in the cottage. 'That's alright,' Peter said, 'we are used to fending for ourselves.'

They were satisfied with the cottage. Bob had put up a couple of beds and blankets. Rosie had left the table and chairs and a few plates and mugs, a frying pan and two saucepans. They had an old motorcycle which Peter rode with Paul sitting behind. When they had settled in, Peter made tea with boiled eggs and bread and butter. They ate in silence for a while, until Paul said, 'That daughter up at the house isn't bad looking.' 'Don't you even look at her!' Peter shouted. 'Any move in that direction and we'll be out. We'll go to Cavan on Saturday nights and I don't care what you do there, but keep your hands off that young girl. I'm warning you!'

Sean soon picked up the work at the factory. A young woman, Susan Kelly, worked with him. He didn't like her very much. She seemed to be beside him every time he turned around, too close, far closer than necessary, he thought. One day she said, 'Barry will be here today.' 'Who's Barry?' Sean asked. 'You know Barry. He delivers the shoe laces.' She smiled a secret little smile. The back door opened and a young man with sandy hair and freckles carried in a large box. He put it down and turned to Susan. 'And how is my favourite girl today?' he smiled, showing perfect white teeth. Susan simpered, 'I'm fine, Barry, how are you?' While this was going on, Sean opened the box and started checking the invoice. 'It's all there Sean,' Barry said. 'I never get an order wrong, do I, sweetheart?' He looked at Susan. 'Well,' Sean said, 'you've got it wrong this time. One box of black and one box of brown, not here.' Sean went out to the van and opened the door. There on the passenger seat were two boxes of laces marked B.12, Wilson's code number. He picked them up and carried them in. Barry started blustering. 'Can't think how that happened, Sean.' Mr Wilson came in then and asked what the trouble was. 'There was two boxes short,' Sean said, 'but Barry found them in the van.'

Mr Wilson took Barry and Susan through to his office. Sean put the order away and wondered what sort of people pulled tricks like that. Susan came back through, picked up her coat and left. Sean didn't know where Barry was. Just before seven, Mr Wilson came through to Sean. 'Good lad,' he said, 'I knew something was happening there, but Susan was in it with him. He admitted he had a hardware shop he sold them to. Susan knew how to check our order, but for a few shillings from Barry she was turning a blind eye.' 'Where is he now?' asked Sean. 'On his way back to the wholesaler, but he's lost his job. He's lucky I didn't hand him over to the Gardai, and Susan, the stupid girl. I learned the trade in a factory in Nottingham. I spent ten years there. I know all there is to know about making shoes and I know all the fiddling that goes on. I hope I never have to catch you, Sean.' 'You won't catch me, sir,' Sean said. 'I hate dishonesty, and my mother would kill me if she ever heard of my doing anything like that.' Mr Wilson smiled. 'And Bob West would help her,' he said.

Chapter 2

Rosie's daughters had settled down well in the convent school in Belturbet. Dennis was attending the Catholic school in Butlersbridge until July and would then go as a boarder to the College in Navan, which was run by the Jesuit Brothers. The three little girls got some teasing from the hard core pupils because they came from the country. The main one was a girl called Connie Kelly, the younger sister of Susan Kelly who worked with Sean in the factory. Connie was smaller than Maura Connolly, who was tall for her age. Connie had four friends, tough like herself. As the three Connollys came up the hill from home, Connie stepped out and said, 'Your bastard of a brother got my sister sacked.' Maura didn't know what to say. Sean hadn't mentioned the scene in the factory to any of his family. Maura, holding her sisters' hands, just looked at Connie and walked on. 'You're country dirt,' Connie shouted. 'Three little bog trotters, eh girls?' Maura turned round, looked Connie up and down and said, 'You look like you have just been dragged out of a bog,' and then walked on. Connie rushed at her from behind and Maura fell in the wet road. The four friends jumped on her and kicked and punched her. Then they turned on the smallest, Nuala and Kathleen, dragging them by their hair and slapping their faces. The little ones began to cry, but Maura got up and, swinging her school satchel, caught Connie on the side of her head. She fell awkwardly and couldn't get up.

Maura walked away with her sisters, but got a ticking-off from the nuns for coming to school dirty and untidy. 'I'm surprised at your mother letting you out like that,' said Sister Theresa. Little Nuala, still crying, said, 'Connie Kelly knocked Maura down, and her friends pulled our hair and hit us.' 'Well, wait till Connie Kelly gets here and I'll have something to say to her,' said Sister Theresa.

Connie and her friends didn't get to school. Connie's leg was broken and she had to go to hospital. Her mother turned up at the school and told a very different story. The Superior had all the girls in her study, together with Rosie and Mrs Kelly. Maura admitted swinging her satchel. 'I couldn't let her beat us and do nothing about it. I didn't know her sister was sacked from the factory and I don't believe Sean would get anyone into trouble, and even if he had, it wasn't my fault.' The Superior listened in silence till they had all talked and then said, 'So that's what this is all about. Susan has been sacked. What did she do, Mrs Kelly? Enlighten us. Mrs Connolly has just lost her husband and we have found her children well behaved and good at their work. I wish I could say the same for your Connie. It's regrettable that she has a broken leg, but Maura has a few bruises coming out too. So let it all finish. Please. Back to classes, children.'

Rosie said, 'I'm sorry about Connie, Mrs Kelly. I've never had any trouble from Maura. She didn't intend Connie any harm, I'm sure.' Mrs Kelly burst into tears. 'I know Connie is difficult,' she said. 'Susan was the same at school, now she's got no work. I don't know what I'm going to do. I've got four young ones.' 'Has your husband got work?' Rosie asked. 'He has, but he likes a drink and backs the horses. I depended on Susan's money.' The Superior listened and knew she couldn't help the Kellys. She also knew that Mrs Kelly liked a drink as well and the children were often left to look after themselves at night. They had got wild and unmanageable. The Connollys were a different story. The three girls were very bright and Dennis and Sean had done well at school. Rosie fed her family well on less money than Mrs Kelly had. Chalk and cheese, these two mothers, she thought.

Chapter 3

Sean came home from work very excited. 'Mr Wilson wants me to go to the Technical College for a whole day each week to learn book-keeping when he can find someone to replace Susan.' 'What will that cost?' Rosie asked. 'He's paying, Mam, and he's paying the bus fare. I will be starting after Easter.'

Maura was wondering how things would be the next day at school, but she found she had many friends—even Connie's mates were nice to her. Anyone who could break Connie Kelly's leg was a hero. When Connie came out of hospital she hobbled up to school on crutches. She met Maura outside the school and said, 'When I get rid of these crutches, you are dead, Maura Connolly!' Maura put her face close to Connie's and said, 'and then I will break your other leg.' Everyone laughed and shouted, 'Hooray, Maura!' Connie hobbled back home, festering with hate. She had lost face, and even her friends had turned against her.

Sean cycled out to their old cottage. It was the end of March, and he wanted to see the Wests. It was a lovely spring day, a Sunday afternoon and the heather on the bog was in bloom looking pretty. He put his bike down and walked along the Pass. He stopped where his father had drowned and, to his amazement found the ground bright with primroses, smelling lovely in the sunshine, and bluebells in bud. He stood and stared. A quiet voice behind him suddenly said, 'Hello, Sean.' Liz West stood there. 'I see you have found my private garden,' she smiled. 'It's lovely,' he said. 'Why, Liz? and when did you plant it?' 'The Sunday after the funeral. I wanted to give Hughie something. I loved him, and I still miss him—and you.' They sat on the grass. 'Mam would be pleased to see this,' Sean said, 'but she says she'll never walk the Pass again, and if she knew I was here she'd have a fit.' 'Come up to the house and see Mam and Dad, they will be pleased to see you,' she said. 'How are the maths, Liz?' 'Don't ask,' she replied. 'I've talked Dad out of sending me to the Royal School in Cavan, but I'm going to start at the Technical College after Easter for shorthand and typing.' 'I'm going to the Tech too,' Sean said. One day a week for book-keeping, but we might see each other there sometimes.'

The Wests were delighted to see Sean and glad to hear that the family were well. Sean told them about Susan, and Maura's row with Connie. 'Were the children picking on your sisters, Sean?' Barbara asked. 'The town children think they are very smart.' 'Not any more,' Sean laughed. 'Maura threatened to break her other leg if she started again, so Nuala told me. The children think Maura's wonderful now.'

Chapter 4

Maura Connolly resolved to never be afraid of anyone again. She had been frightened of Connie Kelly and she had been frightened of the Superior, but she found Connie was as cowardly as the next and the Superior was a very understanding person. So her life became easier. She was eager to learn all she could and hoped to be able to help support her mother. Dennis, the bright one, was going to be a priest and would be studying for years, so no help there. Maura was a plain little girl with straight dark hair and nice teeth. Her large, violet-coloured eyes were her redeeming feature. Kathleen and Nuala were fair-haired and pretty. Sean was tall, fair-haired and very handsome, with blue eyes and a lovely smile. Dennis was the odd one. He was shorter in build and had black curly hair. He looked sullen and didn't smile much. Maura wondered how he would get on in a parish. She also wondered if his heart was in it. He seemed to have been pushed by their parents since he was small, and everyone took it for granted that Dennis would be a priest.

Dennis himself was in some doubt about the priesthood. It wasn't the thought of a celibate life that was the trouble, but he had strong political views about his country, and the British Government ruling Ulster angered him. When he went fishing with Sean one Saturday afternoon, they began to talk about the way their lives were heading. Sean was very happy in his job and he enjoyed his day at the Technical College. He knew he would be moving into the office, away from the stores, and Mr Wilson had told him that he himself was tied down to the office when he wanted to be out drumming up trade. Dennis listened and then said slowly, 'I'm not sure any more. I'd like to get into politics.' Sean stared at him. 'What would you know about politics? You're going to be a priest. Who's been talking to you, turning your head?' 'We have debates at school,' Dennis replied. 'Eamon Maguire, our English teacher, takes the chair and listens to what we've got to say. He's invited me to a meeting tonight.' 'Have you told Mam about this? Christ, Dennis, she will be heartbroken if you don't go to Navan. She has her heart set on you, and she's worked her fingers to the bone. Working class lads like you and me don't become politicians.' Dennis smiled. 'There's politicians and politicians,' he said quietly, 'and Mam will get over it. Don't say anything to her for now.' 'You're damned right I won't tell her. You can do that yourself. I wouldn't want to be in your shoes when you do.'

The long summer holidays were over. Rosie took Dennis into Cavan and bought him new clothes; a nice dark suit and a raincoat, plenty of underwear and a watch. When a new suitcase was packed with loving care, Sean wondered if Dennis had changed his mind once again and was going to Navan. They all walked to the bus stop and waved him off. 'Write soon,' Rosie said, as she hugged him. 'I will, Mam,' he said. 'I will write tomorrow.'

Rosie hummed to herself as she went about her housework. Dennis had been gone three days now. There would be a letter in the post soon, telling her he liked the College and the Brothers, and sending his love to everyone. Hughie would have been proud that she had managed to get the boy to College. Sometimes she felt Hughie was helping her. He seemed so near at times, like the day she slipped and fell in the vegetable garden. She felt Hughie's hand helping her up. She knew people would laugh at her if she told them, so she told no one. A loud knock on the door brought her back to reality. The postman handed her a letter. 'Good', she thought. 'It's from Dennis,' she told the postman. 'He promised to write and he is a man of his word.' She shut the door quickly, eager to hear all his news.

Dear Mam,
I couldn't face the College but I'm alright. I can't give you an
address as I don't know where I'll be. Try to forgive your loving son.
Dennis.

She looked at the postmark—Dublin. What was he doing in Dublin, and why hadn't he said something before he left home? She sat down and put her head on her arms and cried. Hughie, where are you now? I need your help. Dear God, send this stupid boy home and make him explain it to me. But nobody came. An hour later she made herself a cup of tea and was about to drink it when the door opened. Father Brady, the parish priest, walked in looking angry. 'Mrs Connolly, where is Dennis? Why didn't he go to College? I've had a very sharp letter from Brother Hubert.' Rosie silently handed him the letter.

Sean came in, cheerfully slamming the door behind him. Rosie stood at the end of the table, her face like thunder. 'I suppose you knew all about this?' she said. 'All about what?' Sean was puzzled. She tossed the letter across the table. He picked it up and read it. He waited a minute and then said, 'The bloody young fool! He'll never get away. He's committed for life—or what's left of it.' 'What do you mean?' Rosie asked. 'He's joined the IRA, that's what. They'll never let him go. He'll work for them or they will shoot him. That's the way they operate.' 'So you knew!' she shouted. 'You knew, and never said!' 'I didn't know. While we were fishing he said he had been meeting one of the teachers, going to meetings with him, but he took the new clothes and the money you gave him. I really believed he was going to Navan.' 'I've had Father Brady here, he thought Dennis hadn't gone. I showed him the letter. He's as angry with me as he is with Dennis. Don't say anything to the girls in case they tell someone. I don't think Father Brady will talk either. I will tell Bob West when he comes. He won't tell anyone either, but he's bound to ask about Dennis.'

One or two people asked how Dennis was doing. Sean or Rosie would say he was doing fine and slowly people stopped asking. The three girls didn't ask either, as Mam always snapped at them when Dennis was mentioned.

Sean got a good report when the College broke for Christmas and Mr Wilson was pleased with him. Little Patsy was starting school in January. He was a few months short of five, but the nuns agreed to take him. Mr Wilson wanted someone to take Sean's place in the store and asked Rosie if she could do it. She said she would, but only if she worked the school hours. So it was agreed. She gave up the cleaning and working a full day, Monday to Friday. The extra money was a great help.

The Superior asked her to come to the school and, sitting over a cup of tea, told her Maura should be going to college. 'She is very bright and could train as a teacher.' 'She's only fifteen years old,'

Rosie said. 'I know,' was the reply, 'but another year here with us and she will be ready. Can you afford it?' 'Yes. Dennis isn't costing me anything now. What I saved for him, I can save for Maura.' 'I have heard rumours about Dennis. He didn't turn up at Navan, so do you know where he is?' the nun inquired. Poor Rosie shook her head. 'I pray for him every day, but I doubt if I will ever see him again. We had such hopes for him. I remember Hughie telling him he would be a bishop one day, and I think he believed it.'

Chapter 5

Dennis got on the bus and, to his horror, saw some people he knew at the front. He sat near the back and whispered to the conductor, 'Single to Dublin, please.' The people getting off in Cavan said to him, 'You are off to Navan then. Good luck!' The conductor looked puzzled, but decided to mind his own business. It was a four-hour journey. Dennis had been told to go into the bus station cafe and sit at the corner table. He bought tea and a sandwich and presently a smart looking man sat down beside him. He didn't speak while he drank his tea, but then said, 'I take it that you are Dennis?' Dennis nodded, and the man said, 'Come along then.' They walked to the car park and got into a large old car.

There were two boys in the back seat. Dennis crowded in with them. Then another man, whom he hadn't seen, got into the passenger seat. It was dusk, and Dennis couldn't see the signposts, but he guessed they were heading south. They seemed to travel for hours, and the three lads fell asleep. Dennis woke first. They were on a rough track, and presently stopped at a large house. It looked empty, but one of the men had a key and hustled the boys upstairs. There was an older man there, who spoke to them. 'Hello, lads. I expect you are hungry.' They sat on the floor and ate eggs, bacon, sausages and beans, washed down with mugs of tea. The youngest boy, called Barney, said, 'Why are we eating upstairs?' The man answered, 'This house is supposed to be empty. If the Gardai come round and look through the windows downstairs they will see only empty rooms. If they do come round, we will stay quiet and they'll go away. Sorry, you will have to bed down on the floor—and we can't light a candle.' He threw them three sleeping bags and left them.

They were called at five o'clock the next morning and after a bowl of porridge each was taken down to a big barn. Dennis had never seen so many guns. They were stacked carefully in a corner, with straw built around them. There was only a skylight in the roof, no windows in the sides. They were shown how to load and clean the guns and then practised firing at targets. Barney was slow in learning and was told sharply to wake up. Then they did push-ups and other exercises. The car driver put them through their paces, then they were brought back into the house and upstairs, where the other man in the car talked to them. 'Never tell your name or any of your companions' names. Don't speak at all, always look around to see if you are being followed, and don't get mixed up with girls. You won't be going from here for a few weeks. You will be well fed and you can play cards while the light lasts, but we can't risk lighting candles or lamps. If you work hard and get it right, we will take you out on a job or two. Remember, you are doing this for your country. We will get the Brits out of Ulster and have a United Ireland if we work hard, and you will all be heroes. You will go down in the history books like Brian Born and all the other great men who have fought for Ireland. So enjoy your stay—and work hard.'

Barney didn't like being stuck in bed before seven each evening. He decided to get out of it and go home, but he didn't say anything to the others. Dennis heard him crying in his sleeping bag. He felt like crying himself, but he felt committed and went to sleep. Barney asked the older man if they could go to Mass on Sunday. The man laughed. 'I'm afraid not, Barney. Church doesn't rate very high here. People all know each other in the country. They would wonder where you lads came from, and it's not worth the risk.'

During the next couple of weeks Dennis noticed that Barney was often criticised, and actually punished with a hard slap once or twice. One night Dennis lay awake. Barney was restless. Eugene, the other boy, snored softly. Then Dennis heard Barney get out of his sleeping bag, and lay still as Barney crept out of the room. Dennis crept over to the window. The moon was bright. He saw Barney running across the field and then, out of the shadows of the house, he saw the older man running after him. Suddenly the man raised a gun and a shot rang out. Barney fell. 'Jesus Christ'! Dennis thought. 'He's killed Barney! The old bastard, all of them, the rotten bunch! They drove him to try it and now they have killed him!' He crawled back into his sleeping bag, but he couldn't sleep. Eugene slept on. Dennis decided the best thing to do was to keep quiet about what he had seen.

Next morning, Eugene asked, 'Where's Barney?' Dennis said he didn't know, but the old man said, 'Barney decided to leave us. He was too soft and he talked too much.'

A week later, Dennis was told he was wanted for a job. 'Take your gun,' the old man said. He sat in the back seat of a car and saw that they were heading north. At dusk they stopped by a dark wood. A man stepped out of the shadows. Dennis was told to take his gun and go with him. They walked through undergrowth for a couple of miles. 'Where are we going?' Dennis asked at last. 'We are crossing the border,' the man replied. 'We can't go by road. The Brits have road checks, and we can't go by the fields, the soldiers walk there. The soldiers don't like the woods, but I know the way. You will be picked up in a few minutes. Take care of yourself. You are very young. I wish I wasn't taking you, but orders have to be obeyed.'

A car pulled up and Dennis was told to get in the back. He had never seen the driver before. For about five miles they drove along without speaking. Then, in a small village, they reversed into a side street and waited. 'Why have we stopped?' Dennis asked. 'The army patrol goes past here. We will let them pass.' A few minutes later some soldiers walked past, two on each side of the road. When they had gone, the driver drove back down the road they had just come from. He stopped and pointed to a nice semi. 'That house with the white door,' he said. 'Take your gun and knock on the door. When the door opens, shoot him. Go on! I will talk to you later.'

Dennis knocked on the door. A tall young man in vest and trousers opened the door. A little boy in pyjamas clung to his legs. Dennis raised the gun and fired. The man fell back, and blood spouted out as the child fell with him. The child turned in shock to look at Dennis, blood dripping from his blond curls. Dennis ran back to the car. It was already moving. It was all over in 30 seconds, but it felt like an hour. Dennis asked at last, 'Who was he?' An informer,' the man replied. 'We have been watching him for months. You have struck a blow for Ireland, young man. You did well. Next time, don't hang about.' 'What would have happened if his wife had answered the door?' Dennis asked. 'His wife goes to evening classes on Wednesdays. We knew he would be at home with the child.' 'You know them then?' Dennis queried. 'Yes, I know them,' was the answer. Suddenly they pulled off the road into a shady lane. They got out of the car and into another one that drew up beside them, and drove back to where Dennis had been picked up. The same man took him back across the border into the Republic again, where the two men were waiting. As they drove away, the driver said, 'Did you do it, Dennis?' 'Yes, I did it.' 'Good man! Now you are one of us.' Somehow, Dennis didn't feel good. He kept remembering the little blond boy with blood in his hair—and the boy had his little brother Patsy's face. He never thought he would be glad to get back to that smelly room and the dirty sleeping bag. He curled up and tried to stop shaking. At last he slept. Eugene didn't ask him where he had been. His turn would come.

Chapter 6

Liz West had finished her two-year course. She was looking for a job, hopefully in a solicitor's office. Barbara wanted her to stay and help to run the house and farm, but Liz didn't want to stay at home all day. She thoroughly disliked Peter and Paul Kennedy. Peter was gruff and unfriendly, and Paul watched her. She often found him standing behind her, staring at her. She hadn't told her parents, but if she had to stay at home Peter and Paul would have to go.

One Saturday Barbara said to Liz, 'It's my turn to do the church flowers. Take the basket and scissors and cut as many as you can.' Liz was reaching up to cut some roses in the hedge when a sound behind her made her turn around sharply and the scissors caught Paul's cheek. A long, deep scratch started bleeding. 'What do you want?' Liz demanded. 'How dare you sneak up behind me? Don't you dare touch me, do you hear? I will tell my father. I hope he sacks you.' 'I will tell him about you meeting that Sean Connolly on the Pass. Sitting on the grass with him, his hands all over you! You, a good Protestant girl, lying in the grass with a Papist. He won't like it.' He leered at her, rubbing his bleeding cheek with a grimy handkerchief. 'My father knows Sean. He used to work here, he owns the cottage you live in. He might consider throwing you and your father out. Think about it before you start accusing me. Sean is my best friend, always has been, and always will be. His whole family are our friends.' 'What—even the one that works with the IRA? Dennis, the bright one—nearly became a priest, didn't he?' 'Just you keep your evil tongue in your cheek. No one knows where he is or what he's doing. Anyway, he's worth ten of you!' Liz turned and walked away.

She and Sean had got into the habit of meeting on the Pass. They had planted more flowers there and clipped the grass. Sometimes they sat and talked. Once, when she cried, Sean had held her and let her cry on his shoulder. She realised that Paul must have followed her and watched—a 'Peeping Tom'. She decided to tell her father. He would understand. Her gentle, kind father who helped everyone.

After tea, Barbara left to go to the church and Bob sat sipping a third cup of tea. Liz didn't know where to start. 'Dad,' she said, 'I wish you would get rid of Peter and Paul.' 'Why?' he asked, surprised. 'Paul watches me all the time. He crept up behind me and I scratched him with the scissors.' 'Did he touch you?' 'No, I heard a noise and I swung round and the scissors caught his cheek, he was that near me. I'm afraid of him, Dad. He is weird. He gives me the creeps.' 'I will talk it over with your Mother tonight. I want you to be happy, not living in fear.' He leaned over and kissed her.

That Saturday night, Peter and Paul got on their motorcycle and went into Cavan. Peter headed for his favourite pub and Paul stopped to speak to a skinny young girl who stood near the pub. 'I need to talk to you,' she whispered. 'What about?' he asked. 'I think I'm pregnant.' 'And what's that to do with me?' he snapped. 'Paul, I've never been with anyone else,' she said, 'and I love you.' 'Go away, you silly bitch!' He slapped her face. 'What do you expect me to do about it?' Her nose trickled blood and she wiped it on the sleeve of her shabby coat. 'What am I going to tell my Da?' she cried. 'I'm only fourteen years old.' 'Ah, tell him what you like!' Paul walked into the pub and left her.

Half an hour later, a small man, neatly dressed, came into the pub. He looked around. 'Which one of you is Paul Kennedy?' he asked. 'Who wants to know?' Peter turned and looked at him with contempt. 'I'd like a word with him,' the man said quietly. 'Well, I'm his father. This is Paul. We will talk outside.'

They followed him out. The young girl stood shivering by the door. Just as the door closed, Peter hit the man. He fell down. Paul aimed a kick at his ribs and the girl ran to her father. Paul grabbed her hair and kicked her. The other people in the pub came out and one rushed to find the Gardai while another called an ambulance. Peter and Paul were handcuffed as they tried to fight the Gardai. The pub owner said later, 'I knew the first time I saw them that they were trouble.'

Bob West answered the door on Sunday morning. Two Gardai stood there. 'Can we have a word, Mr West?' 'Certainly, come in.' They followed him into the kitchen where Barbara and Liz were finishing the breakfast. Barbara jumped up, startled. 'What's wrong? Is it Robert?' she asked. 'No, Mrs West, I'm sure Robert is fine. Sorry to interrupt your breakfast. We've got two of your workers banged up in the cells.' 'The Kennedys?' Bob asked 'Right, the Kennedys,' the older officer answered. He told them what had happened outside the pub. 'Ah, that poor wee girl,' Barbara said, looking at Liz. 'Well,' the officer continued, 'we have questioned them all night. It seems it's not their first time in the cell. Peter did ten years a long time ago and Paul did six months for beating up a young lad about three years ago.' 'What did Peter do to get ten years?' Bob asked. 'He beat up his boss when he was caught stealing. The poor man died two years later. He had brain damage. He should have got life, but the man lived for two years and they couldn't try him again.'

'What about the man last night?' Liz asked. 'He's in hospital, a broken jaw and several broken ribs. How long have they worked here?' 'Just over two years,' Bob said. 'Barbara has never liked them, and Liz was begging me to get rid of them just last night.' 'Why was that, Liz?' the officer asked. 'Paul kept watching me, and following me. He was standing behind me when I was cutting the roses. I turned round and the scissors caught his cheek he was so close to me.' 'Ah,' the officer said. 'He told us the young girl attacked him and scratched his face. We didn't believe it. She is only fourteen and small for her age. Where did they live?' 'Up in Connolly's old cottage,' Bob said.

'We would like to take a look in the house.' 'I will come with you,' Bob said and they started off to the cottage.

Bob never saw such filth in his life. Rotten food, sour milk, ashes piled high in the fire place, dirty shirts trodden into the floor, and the smell was horrible. Under one on the beds was a pile of obscene magazines. All round the bed were pictures of naked women. 'This is awful,' he said. 'I've never seen anything like it.' In the other bedroom there was a bicycle, several spades, rakes and hoes. 'I suppose,' the officer said, 'these are yours?' 'Yes,' Bob replied. 'They are all mine. I wondered where they had gone. What would he have wanted them for?' 'Oh, this sort has to take whatever they find,' the officer said. 'You'd think ten years would have taught him something.'

Later that day, Sean Connolly came with his mother, Rosie. They had heard what had happened. Bob said, 'Rosie, your cottage is in a terrible mess.' 'I will clean it up,' Barbara said. 'No,' said Sean and

Bob together. 'It's not fit for a woman to see,' Sean said. 'I will go up and I'll take everything out and burn the lot—beds, tables, chairs, everything.' 'That's best,' Bob said. 'I'll come with you, Sean. I'll lend you some old things to wear, or you will ruin your good clothes.'

They worked for three hours. Sean was glad his mother hadn't seen the mess. When they finished, Bob said, 'I'll ask the Larkin twins to come in and wash the walls and paint it all out.' 'I would do it,' Sean said, 'but I am only free on Sundays.' 'I'm hoping the Larkins will come and work for me,' Bob said. 'They are sixteen now, and I hear they are looking for work.'

Peter and Paul went to trial a week later. Peter got fifteen years with hard labour and Paul got ten years for grievous bodily harm and for having sex with a minor. Bob West thanked his lucky stars that he hadn't had to sack them—two dangerous men. His family had been in danger for over two years, particularly Liz. He shuddered to think about it. Perhaps there was an angel guarding them. Rosie always said, 'The Wests are the best.' It made him blush whenever she said it. He always replied, 'We just do the best we can.'

Chapter 7

Dennis had begun to think that he would be in the old farm-house for the rest of his life. He had never been told the old man's name, nor the names of the men who had brought him here, but one evening, out of the blue, both men turned up. Dennis was frightened. Not another killing, he prayed. He couldn't face that again. Eugene had been out all night on one occasion and Dennis knew in his heart that poor Eugene had been through the same drama that he had. But they didn't talk much, just exercised in the barn, target practice and sleeping. Now, Dennis was told to have a bath and wash his hair. Most of his new clothes were still in the case.

The next morning, dressed in his best and with his suitcase in the boot, he was driven off. As they drove along he was told he was going to Dublin to apply for work. He was told the job was in a big warehouse and he would have to fill in an application form. Digs had been found for him. They stopped at a barber's shop and he had his hair cut; were they letting him go? he wondered. However, he was shown into a large office and the receptionist told him to take a seat. Five young men of about his own age were already seated. Presently, a young man came in from an inner office and handed each one a form, which asked about their age, religion, school reports, and had various other general knowledge questions. Dennis answered it carefully. What was his last job? Dennis thought hard about it and finally wrote down that he worked for a year with his uncle, a farmer in Limerick. Each one was interviewed and Dennis got the job. His digs were with a widow and her daughter. His room was comfortable and the food was good. He was to have a salary of twenty pounds per month, £6 of which was for his digs. He had been given five pounds to tide him over, and he still had the money Rosie had given him, so he paid a month's rent in advance and had a bit to spare.

He hadn't realised what a big concern the company was. B.J. Williams, Importers and Exporters, had a huge building and about two hundred workers. Dennis was working with an older man, a kindly man with a lot of patience. He told Dennis he had worked there for twenty-five years. Dennis was smart and learned fast, and found his voice in the staff room at tea breaks. He had been teased because he was so quiet, but he couldn't tell them about the year he had lived in near silence at the old farmhouse. He decided it was time to write to his mother.

He thought about his family a lot—Maura, Kathleen, little Nuala and Patsy, and again he would see the little blond boy with his curls dripping with blood. The boy he had left fatherless. He hoped he would never have to do it again. So he sat down and tried to compose a letter to Rosie. He told her where he was working and the address of his lodgings. He asked her to forgive him—and could he come home some time and see them all? He sent his love to the girls and Patsy, and asked how Sean was. He put a pound note in the letter and posted it.

Chapter 8

Rosie met the postman as she was leaving for work. She had hoped and prayed for news of Dennis. Now the letter was in her hand, and she was afraid to read it. She stuffed it into her pocket and went to work. As soon as she got time, she went through to Sean and asked him to read it first. Sean did so, and handed it back. 'Don't worry, Mam,' he said. 'He is working in Dublin and he has digs in the city. He has put his address at the top so you can write to him.'

Sean had his own thoughts about Dennis. What had he being doing for a whole year? Learning to kill, he supposed, and probably *had* killed. He hoped Dennis would stay away. He didn't want to have trouble with terrorists. The Connollys were going well. Enough money was coming in to keep them, with a bit to save. Maura was going to start the Tech in September and then on to Teacher Training College. Sean was proud of himself and his family. He looked at his mother and thought how lovely she was. She had lost weight, and her long fair hair was coiled neatly at the back of her neck. Under her overall she wore a slim black skirt and white blouse. Her skin was clear and her cheeks rosy. He wondered if she would marry again; he hoped so. She deserved a happy life.

The young woman they rented the cottage from had built a bathroom and flush toilet. She had had to put up the rent but they would manage and the bathroom was great. No more filling the tin bath in front of the fire on Saturday. Sean had bought an electric cooker as well, so life was easier all round. Living on the edge of the town had its advantages, Rosie decided. Electric light and an immersion heater for the water, with an airing cupboard. Even the Wests were envious; the Electricity Board hadn't reached them yet. Liz West often called in at weekends, her large blue eyes following Sean everywhere. Rosie worried about this. He never bothered with girls, but his face lit up when Liz called, and she knew he often rode his bike out to the Wests on Sundays. Nothing would ever come of it. Sean was a good Catholic and Liz a Protestant. It had no future, Rosie thought, no future at all.

Rosie sat down and tried to compose a letter to Dennis. She thought Sean was wrong after all. Dennis would never join the Provos. He was educated and sensible. She told him she forgave him, but if he had not wanted to go to the Jesuit College he should have told her. Running away never solved anything. He could come home any time he liked. The girls and Patsy sent their love, and she was glad he was working and had good digs, and thanked him for the pound.

Chapter 9

Dennis was having a sandwich and a coffee in a little cafe near his work one day when a man came and sat with him. It was the man he had privately called 'Red', because of his hair. 'Well, Dennis, how are you getting on?' he asked. 'Alright,' Dennis answered. 'There's a little job I'd like you to do for me,' the man said. 'No, not another killing!' Dennis was horrified. 'No, no,' he was told, 'nothing like that.' Dennis waited. 'There's a great iron gate at the back of the warehouse and another door leading into the building.' 'That's right,' Dennis said, 'and they are both kept locked most of the time.' You know where the keys are kept?' 'Yes, in the office cupboard.' The man took two flat tin boxes from his pocket. 'When you get the chance, put a key in each of these boxes. Press down hard and then lift the keys out. Wipe them clean and put them back. Now, that's not difficult is it?' 'No,' Dennis said, 'but why?' 'Don't worry about it. Just do it. Don't let anyone see you, and bring the boxes back to me a week today.'

The man moved away and disappeared into the busy street. Dennis put the boxes into his pocket. He didn't understand any of it, but he began to see why this job had been found for him. In the privacy of his room he opened the boxes and found they were filled with plasticine. Two days later, when he was alone in the office, he quickly did as he had been instructed, put the boxes back in his pocket and only opened them when he got home. There were two perfect impressions of the gate keys. At last, he knew they were going to raid the office and the warehouse. He handed the boxes over on the appointed day and waited in dread, but nothing happened.

As he sat having his lunch one day, watching people queuing up, he saw a tall young man. He tried to remember who he was, or where he had seen him before. The young man came and sat at his table and, as they looked at each other, Dennis exclaimed, 'Robert West!' 'Hello, Dennis.' Robert smiled at him. 'I have seen you in here before, but today I decided to say hello. I have been working at the Baggot Street hospital since Christmas and I've just slipped out to get a birthday card for my mother.'

Robert wanted to know where he worked, and was impressed by how smart Dennis looked. 'Come out for a meal with me, Dennis, and we can have a talk about the families tomorrow night. I will book a table and meet you here first.' So it was agreed. It was a good restaurant. The food was excellent. Dennis had never tasted food like it and Robert talked about home. Dennis heard about Sean being Assistant Manager and Rosie working in the stores and Maura starting Technical College. Liz was staying at home and helping to run the farm. He was told about the pranks and fun the Larkin twins were having, although they were working well, Bob said.

All in all it was a pleasant evening, and they left the restaurant at ten o'clock. Robert called a taxi and dropped Dennis off at his lodgings, where the landlady and daughter wanted to know what he had had to eat, and after a cup of coffee Dennis went to bed. Eating his breakfast the next morning, the radio stopped for a news flash,' 'B.J. Williams in Curzon Street was raided last night. The night watchman was badly beaten and tied up. The safe was blown up and about ten thousand pounds in cash and cheques were taken. The Gardai do not know how the thieves got in. The gates were locked when the first workers arrived at seven o'clock.'

Dennis hurried to work. He knew all the staff would be questioned. Thank God he had an alibi. He had spent the evening with Robert West. When he arrived at work he was stopped at the door by a Garda. 'You can't go in there,' he was told. 'But I work here,' he replied. 'Your name, please?' 'Dennis Connolly.' 'How long have you worked here?' 'Seven months and a few days.'

He was taken into the staff room, where several other members of staff were sitting nervously. 'What happened?' Dennis asked. 'I heard some of it on the radio. They said the night man was beaten up. Who was it?' 'Old William, we think. He is in hospital. The Gardai are waiting with him to question him,' a young typist told him.

Each of them was taken separately and questioned. Dennis said he had been out with a young doctor called Robert West, who worked in the Baggot Street hospital. They had been brought up together and had met by chance one day in the cafe. They had taken a taxi back. Robert had dropped him off at his digs. He had had a coffee with his landlady and gone to bed at about 11 o'clock. The Gardai said they would check out his story. Everyone had an alibi.

The Gardai were baffled. On Thursday night all the wages were in the safe. Did the thieves get lucky? On Friday night the safe would have been empty, as all money was banked on Friday. Or had the thieves an accomplice inside who had given them that information?

By the end of the day they were all back at their places, but the Gardai were still there, looking for fingerprints or the weapon used to beat old William, but nothing was found. William died in the night. His old heart couldn't stand the shock of such a beating, so he was never able to tell anything. Sean heard it on the radio in the office and thought, 'Our Dennis knows something about this'. But he couldn't tell anyone as he couldn't prove anything, and he didn't want to get involved. He had to think of Rosie and the children.

Chapter 10

Gareth Nesbitt sat in his apartment in Belgrave Square. He wanted to be alone. He smiled grimly. He was always alone, but he needed a lonely place. He had decided to write his book. He wanted his life on paper.

He was the only child of Mildred and Roger Nesbitt. His father had been a bank manager before he retired and his mother had belonged to everything in the village of Eastbrook—the Women's Institute, Mothers' Union, Wives Groups—and she sang in the choir. Gareth had a lonely childhood. They had a live-in maid when he was young and he spent most of his school holidays with his grandmother. He loved her. Her little house was cosy, she had plenty of books and she never nagged him. His mother used to say, 'Why don't you play football or cricket, like the other boys? When you go to Winchester you will have to play games.' Gareth had long ago made up his mind he wouldn't go to Winchester.

When he was ten he told his parents he wanted to live with his grandmother, and after a lot of to-ing and fro-ing he was allowed to live with her and attend the local secondary school. He went on to the sixth Form College and when he was 18 his grandmother died. He had always believed she owned her house, but she had rented it. She left £2,000 to Gareth in her will and the furniture and jewellery to be sold to pay for her funeral. So, Gareth packed his bags and took the train to London. He found a bed-sit which suited him and a job in a bookshop.

He was very happy at work. The owner went to auctions and house sales, sometimes picking up first editions and very old books. They also did a brisk trade in modem books, and the window was always full of new writers as well as old classics. Mrs Ward, a woman in her fifties, was always there. She was an authority on books, old and new, and Gareth worked with her.

One day Gareth came back after lunch to find a handsome man sitting drinking tea with Mrs Ward. The man looked up and smiled. 'Who have we here, Mrs Ward?' he asked, rising from his chair. 'This is Gareth Nesbitt,' she answered. 'Gareth, this is Sir Guy Mallorey, a very good customer of ours.' Sir Guy held out his hand and Gareth took it. It was a warm handshake, and Sir Guy held his hand for a second longer than necessary. Mrs Ward spoke. 'Gareth is a great bookworm.' 'Well, you must come round to my apartment. I've got a few treasures.' 'I'd love to,' Gareth replied, 'thank you.'

Gareth hoped Sir Guy would come in again, as he felt strangely attracted to the older man. Two days later Sir Guy rang. Gareth answered the call and was invited to come to dinner that evening. He wondered if he would be the only guest, and worried if he was dressed properly.

He rang the bell and the door was answered by an elderly butler. Sir Guy greeted him warmly, again holding his hand. The butler brought in a tray with sherry glasses and a couple of decanters and left them. Sir Guy asked him about his family and Gareth told him he didn't see them very often. 'I've been a great disappointment to them,' Gareth said, 'but I am what I am.' They ate a beautifully served dinner and looked at some books and drank coffee. Sir Guy told him the butler and his wife looked after him, but lived out. 'They are a treasure,' he said. 'It's hard to find good servants these days. They have been with me for years.'

Gareth was invited again and again, and on one occasion, when Sir Guy kissed him goodbye, Gareth wasn't surprised. He was growing very fond of him and he was rather pleased. One night when Gareth was ready to go home, the butler handed him his coat. Sir Guy stood there, and as the door opened the wind blew snow into the hall. 'It's a terrible night,' Sir Guy said, 'why don't you stay the night?' So Gareth stayed, and when Sir Guy later walked hand in hand with him into the bedroom, it seemed quite natural for Gareth to get into the lovely four-poster bed with him.

So began a lifelong friendship. Sir Guy wanted to take a world cruise and asked Gareth to go with him. He handed in his notice at the bookshop and had the time of his life. A year later they went to Ireland and Sir Guy drove his fast car all over the country, staying at grand hotels or sometimes small bed and breakfast places. Gareth never felt he was being kept. He had his grandmother's money. He sent a postcard to his parents sometimes, but he never mentioned Sir Guy. Sometimes they lived in London, sometimes on Sir Guy's estate in Wiltshire. When he wanted to entertain, Sir Guy rang anyone of the ladies he knew and she would act as hostess. They all would have liked to marry him, but he smilingly told them they were worthy of better and kissed their hands. Gareth sometimes felt a twinge of jealousy when the ladies hung on his arm, but he knew Sir Guy forgot them as soon as they left.

Then, after about 15 years, Sir Guy didn't feel well. He saw his doctor and was referred to a specialist. He was told he had cancer of the liver. He had a lot of treatment in London and in America, but became very ill. Gareth nursed him and looked after him, changing his sheets and holding him when he vomited. Sir Guy protested, 'Let me go into hospital. You shouldn't be doing this,' but Gareth, with tears running down his face, said, 'I want to look after you. I have always loved you, all these fifteen years I have been so happy, and I hope you have been. I don't want strangers touching you.'

At last Sir Guy died. He had a sister he hadn't seen for twenty years who was married to a Conservative MP. Guy left her the estate in Wiltshire and left his apartment to Gareth, together with his money—so much money Gareth didn't know how to handle it. He got the bank to invest it and drew an allowance each month. Guy's sister tried to break the will, but couldn't. Guy had made it ten years previously, when his health had been good.

He was buried in the churchyard in Wiltshire, with his family, and Gareth left as soon as he could. He went back to London, trying to make some sense of his life without Guy. He rang the airport and booked a flight to Dublin. He asked the butler and his wife to look after the apartment and arranged their pay.

He arrived in Dublin with no plans. He booked into a small hotel and finally decided to buy a car. He found a small Austin, two years old. He looked it over. Guy had taught him a few things about running a car. He got out the road map of Ireland and, closing his eyes, stuck a pen into the map. He had picked a town called Belturbet in County Cavan. He had never heard of it—but so be it, he thought. Belturbet it is.

After getting out of the busy Dublin traffic he found himself travelling through the beautiful countryside of County Meath. The fields were lush, and sheep grazed on the hillside. After two and a half hours he arrived in Cavan town. Where to now? A young man with a suitcase stood by a bus stop. He pulled up and asked the way to Belturbet. 'I'm going there,' the lad said, 'I'm waiting for the bus.' 'Well, hop in! We will travel together.'

Dennis wondered what an Englishman with a high class accent wanted Belturbet for, but he was making his first journey back home after two years and wasn't sure what sort of a reception he would get. 'Is there a hotel in Belturbet?' Gareth asked. 'There's two,' Dennis replied, 'but I'd say the Railway Hotel would be more your sort. A bit better class than Clancy's. That's more of a pub.' 'Oh right, I'll be looking for a place out in the country to rent after I've had a look around.' 'There's no mod cons in the country places,' Dennis said. 'No water or electricity. I mean the water is in the well, and you'd need candles or paraffin lamps. You might be better in the town.' Gareth didn't reply. 'This is a funny bugger,' Dennis thought.

On the outskirts of the town Dennis asked Gareth to let him out. 'That little cottage is my home,' he said. 'Whether I'll be welcome is another matter.' 'Why is that?' Gareth asked. 'It's a long story. If we meet again I will tell you. Follow this road until you reach the Town Hall, it stands in the middle of The Diamond. Turn left and you will come to the Railway Hotel.'

Gareth shook his hand. 'Good luck,' he said. 'And you,' Dennis answered.

Dennis walked slowly up the path. He knocked on the door. Maura opened it. 'Dennis!' she shouted. 'Kathleen, Nuala, look, it's our Dennis!' She hugged him. 'Where's Mam?' he asked. 'She will be here in a minute. She works now. She's up at the factory. So is Sean. He's Assistant Manager now.' Nuala was so excited she was tripping over her tongue. 'I met Robert West in Dublin. He told me all the news.'

Dennis wondered what his mother would say, but he needn't have worried. Rosie was standing at the door beaming at him, her arms held out. He went to her and hugged her. 'Tea's nearly ready,' Maura said. 'Sean will be in soon.' 'Where's Patsy?' Dennis asked. 'He's playing football,' Rosie said, 'He's football mad.' 'I didn't think he was old enough to play,' Dennis remarked. 'He's seven now, but he is still baby-faced and he doesn't like his curls being cut.' Sean came in, followed by Patsy. They all sat down to tea. Dennis told them about his work and his lodgings and about the night out with Robert West. 'That was the night the warehouse was raided. I couldn't believe it. The whole place was so secure.' 'Did they catch the thieves?' Sean asked. 'No,' said Dennis. 'They will be long gone by now. It's over six months ago. Poor old William died. That was a shame, he was a nice old fellow.'

Sean watched Dennis's face as he talked, and thought, 'He's either a great actor or he's not guilty'. Dennis then told them about the Englishman who had given him a lift from Cavan, and that he was looking for an isolated cottage and that he was staying at the Railway Hotel. 'I told him,' said Dennis, 'that he would be better off near the town. The old country cottages have no electric or water, and I don't think he would know how to light a fire and cook on it.' 'I hear you are starting Tech in September, Maura.' 'Yes,' said Rosie, 'she has gone from strength to strength since she started at the Convent. Now Sister Jane Maeve tells me that Kathleen has done some great drawings and beautiful sewing.'

Kathleen ran and fetched her drawing book, ladies dressed in flowing dresses and a beautiful bride with bridesmaids. They reminded Dennis of the fashion shops in Dublin. 'These are great,' Dennis exclaimed, 'just like the expensive shops in Grafton Street. Could you make these clothes?' 'I won't know until I try. I could find out if I had a sewing machine,' Kathleen said. Rosie smiled. 'You shall have one, I promise you. I'm proud of you all. I wish your father could see you now.' Nuala said, 'Dad *can* see us. He looks after us all. How else would we be as well as we are? Of course he knows, and he's as proud as you are.'

Dennis stayed at home for a week and Sean couldn't find fault with him. When Rosie and Sean went to work, and the others were at school, Dennis tidied the house and washed up. He mowed the grass and weeded the flower bed in front. Walking through the town, he saw Gareth Nesbitt go into the bank.

Gareth arranged with the manager to have his income paid into the bank each month. He told the manager he wanted a quiet cottage where he could write in peace. 'Why did you pick this place?' he was asked. 'I closed my eyes and picked it with a pen, and decided to stick with it.' 'There's a cottage out near Rabulton. There are no services there and you have to cross a dangerous bog Pass.' 'I'd like to see it.' 'The owner lives in the white cottage out on the Cavan Road.' 'I gave a young man a lift yesterday. He didn't tell me his name, but he went in there.' 'Well, you will find Mrs Connolly and her family there after five o'clock. They will show it to you, I'm sure.'

Gareth thanked the manager and walked around the town. He liked it. It had some useful shops and a beautiful bridge over the River Erin. He stood and watched the water for a while, then wandered back to the hotel. He sat reading until six o'clock, then drove to the Connollys.

Sean answered the door and Gareth asked to speak to Mrs Connolly. 'Come in,' Sean said. Rosie stood beside the table, pouring tea. All her family sat round. Gareth said, 'Perhaps I should come back. I'm interrupting your meal.' 'Not a bit of it,' Rosie said, 'sit down and drink a cup of tea.' 'Well, hello again.' Gareth smiled at Dennis. 'Hello to you,' Dennis said. Gareth explained that the bank manager had told him that Rosie had an empty cottage in the country. 'I'd like to see it with the aim of renting it.' 'There's a dangerous bog Pass to reach it' Rosie said. 'I doubt if you could get a car up there.' 'Well, could I just look? If I like it, I'll have the Pass surfaced and fenced off, if you would like that.' 'I can't afford all that work,' Rosie said. 'I wouldn't dream of letting you pay for it. I'll see to it, if I like the house.' Nuala spoke. 'Why do you want to live out there? It's foggy in winter and the nearest neighbours, Wests, live two fields away.' 'I want to write a book. It will take a long time. If I get it finished I might write another one.'

He looked around the table at the children. What a brave woman this was, he thought. The little boy looked like a cherub with his golden hair curling around his head. The girls' hair was neatly braided and Maura, with her brown hair shoulder length, was so tall and dignified, like a lady of quality, he thought. This was a special family. He hoped he would be around to watch them develop.

Gareth drove with Sean beside him to look at the cottage. It was a bright evening, and although it was nearly 7 o'clock it was sunny and warm. 'Don't take the car up the Pass,' Sean advised. 'I haven't been all the way along, but we might get stuck. It's not far to walk.' They parked the car on the side of the road. The grass had grown high along the Pass and it was difficult to keep to the path, but Sean led the way. They came to the spot where Hughie had drowned, and Gareth looked in wonder at this little oasis, a trim green patch bright with forget-me-nots and pansies. Sean told him, 'That's where my father died. Liz West started putting flowers on the spot and I thought it was a lovely idea, so I helped her. She is the daughter of Bob West. My family worked for the Wests for years and years. They have been good friends.'

They walked on and up the hill and there stood the cottage, snowy white, with a blue door and window frames. A red climber rose grew near the door and had been trained along the wall. Gareth was enchanted by it. It looked so homely. It was small inside, two bedrooms, one each side of the living room. A range stood in the fireplace. The walls were white on the inside and it was very clean. The quarry-tiled floor was clean and shiny. The bedroom floors were wooden and had been scrubbed almost white. The roof was tiled and seemed sound and rainproof. Gareth wanted it. He would have bought it, but agreed to rent it. As they drove back into town, Sean told him about the family, his work, and Rosie and Maura doing well and ready for Tech, and little Kathleen, with her flair for fashion and all the fashion magazines she bought with her pocket money. 'What about Dennis?' Gareth asked. 'I am not happy about Dennis. He got into bad company. He was going to be a priest, but he went to Dublin, disappeared for a year and then turned up in a good job, well dressed and money in his pocket. I'll be glad when he goes back to Dublin. He's my brother, but I feel that things are not quite right. Do you know what I mean, Mr Nesbitt? I'm uneasy with him. I can't help it.' 'Could you call me Gareth, please, Sean? 'I'm not used to being called Mr Nesbitt.' 'Alright, it's Sean and Gareth from now on.'

Gareth started looking for furniture on Monday morning. He found a second-hand furniture shop and bought an old oak dresser, a table and four chairs and two big armchairs. He bought a new bed, blankets and sheets; a few pots and a frying pan; cups, saucers and dinner plates. The man in the shop showed him a Calor gas cooker, with two rings and a grill, and an oven and two gas bottles. Gareth thought it would save him lighting the fire while the weather was warm, so he bought the lot. By the end of the week he had moved in. He had gone to see the Wests and arranged to buy his milk, eggs and butter. He had engaged a firm to fence off the Pass and some quarrymen to make the Pass sound underneath. In the meantime, his car was in West's hay-yard.

He bought a typewriter and practised on it. He was a bit slow, but he preferred it to writing by hand and sat at the table trying to make a start on his book.

He asked the men who were putting up the wire fence along the Pass to put a little gate by the spot where the flowers were. The men thought he was a bit simple, but they did it anyway. Liz West leaned on the garden wall and watched the men working. She thought she wouldn't be able to look after her secret garden, that she was fenced out. It had meant a lot to her during the past two and a half years and she knew that, because it was her and Sean's secret place, that was why it meant so much to her.

She had acknowledged to herself that although she loved Sean, and knew he loved her, that was as far as it could ever go. Marriage was out of the question and Sean had to help support his sisters. She could see herself in years to come working and running this small farm, when really she didn't love the place at all.

It was better since Peter and Paul went, and the Larkin twins were so lively even her serious Mother had to laugh at the two young lads. Their witty tongues and corny jokes made life better for poor Liz. One was called Pat and the other one John. Only their mother, a widow, could tell one from the other. When Barbara asked them their names they both said, 'We are Pat and John. Call either name and one of us will come.' They had led their schoolteacher a merry dance and she finally gave up. They were harmless really, and had had a secret language of their own since they were three years old. However, their mother was a strong, tough woman who had made them work and taught them good manners, and she still kept them in order even though they had turned seventeen.

Gareth asked Barbara West if she knew anyone who could do his laundry, and Mrs Larkin said she would. He paid her well, and always had a good supply of shirts, socks and underwear. He practically lived in jeans and sweaters. Looking at his lovely suits and dinner jackets, he wondered if he would ever need them again. His life had changed, but not the way he had intended.

He had always imagined being on his own, reading and writing all day, but he found he was quite busy. He walked to the little shop every morning and bought a newspaper, calling at the Wests on the way back to collect his can of milk. He cleaned his house and cooked one main meal each day. He started clearing the vegetable garden which the Kennedys had let go wild. He planted spring cabbage and sowed some broad beans. He cleared the weeds out of the rest, ready for spring.

He sawed up logs for his fire in the winter and bought peat from Bob West. Some days he never touched the typewriter and was too tired in the evening to do anything except read. He thought about Guy and wondered if he was laughing at his rustic life, but Guy had been a kind, gentle person who never laughed at anyone. He wrote to his parents and his mother wrote back, demanding to know what he was doing in the middle of a bog in Ireland. 'Why don't you come home and settle?' she wrote. 'You are forty-five years old, with no wife or children and no grandchildren for us.' Gareth smiled as he read it. She hasn't changed, he thought, and she would never understand.

Maura Connolly started at the Technical College in September. She was sixteen years old and very determined to do well. She became friendly with a girl called Caroline Jones, who was also hoping to get to Teacher Training College. They were totally different. Caroline was a big girl, with square shoulders, and taller than Maura. She was very lively because she lived nearly sixty miles away, so she had lodgings in Cavan with a family called Murray. Ted Murray was a chemist, as was Caroline's father. They lived in a nice detached house half a mile out of Cavan. They had two sons, both adults, one in the Army and the other at Leeds University. They were very happy to have Caroline and hoped she would behave. It was worrying having a sixteen-year-old girl. The girls never missed classes, but sometimes they had an hour or two free time and Caroline walked the streets of Cavan attracting the boys from College, or anyone else who took her fancy. She was a born flirt. Poor Maura was tongue-tied. She hadn't spoken to any strange young man in her life and she hadn't a clue what to say to them.

The two girls had a favourite little cafe where they went for a cup of tea. One day, two students that they knew by sight came in and carried their cups of tea over to the girls' table. 'Can we sit with you?' one asked. Caroline smiled up at them. 'It's a free country,' she said, 'sit down.' They talked, or rather Caroline talked, directly to the older boy, called Terry. They were cracking together, like old friends. Maura listened and smiled, and the other boy watched her. His name was Ken, a shy boy with ginger hair and freckles. Maura noticed that his bare arms were freckled too. She thought he had a nice smile, and liked him better than Terry, who was full of himself.

After they all walked back to College together, it became a habit to meet in the tea shop. Caroline tried to get out in the evening to meet Terry, but she wasn't allowed. She told the Murrays she often went out in the evening at home, but Ted rang her father who said, 'No, she doesn't go out in the evening—and if she gets troublesome, she will have to come home.'

Caroline was furious and moaned and groaned to Maura, who laughed at her. 'What would you do if you got out?' she asked.

'Terry has a car. We could go out into the country, perhaps to Belturbet, and he could bring Ken. We could all go out together.'

Maura shook her head. 'I like Ken, but I don't want to go out with anyone and I wouldn't be allowed. My mother would worry, and Sean would want to know where I'd been and what I'd done. No, Caroline, I don't think we ought to take up with the boys; perhaps when we get to Training College. We will be older then.' But Caroline refused to be beaten and on several occasions slipped quietly out of the house when the family were asleep, returning at three o'clock in the morning. She told Maura, who wondered how she could take the risk and what would happen if she was caught.

All this went on until Christmas. Caroline went home for the holiday and, when College started again in January, was desperate to see Terry. Ken told them Terry had gone to England with his brother. Caroline cried, and told Maura she was pregnant. She had told Terry before the holidays, and now she didn't know what to do. 'Well, you will have to tell someone,' Maura said. 'You can't hide it forever. Go home at the weekend and tell your mother, or write and tell her if you can't face her. I can't help you, Caroline. I wish I could.' She helped Caroline to write the letter and made sure she posted it. Caroline's parents arrived to take her home. They were angry with the Murrays for allowing her to run wild, although they protested that she hadn't been out. But Caroline broke down and said she had slipped out after bedtime, and told them that Terry had gone away.

Caroline was sent to stay with an aunt in Donegal and her baby was put up for adoption. She wrote to Maura and seemed to be heartbroken. Maura wrote her a cheerful letter, but never heard from her again.

She hoped Caroline would get a fresh start and learn something from her experience. She shuddered to think if it had happened to her. But it hadn't, and it wouldn't. She hoped some day to marry, but not for ages.

Dennis was having lunch in his usual place when Red came over with a cup of tea and sat down. 'Where have you been then?' he asked. 'I went home to see my family,' Dennis answered. 'How were they all then?' 'Fine, just fine.' Dennis wondered what was coming next.

He soon found out. 'I'll pick you up after you finish tonight,' Red said. 'Another killing?' No, not for you, but I want you to come along.'

That night they drove across the border and into Armagh. They stopped and picked up a lad of about eighteen. Dennis knew he was carrying a gun. This eager young lad, eager to fight for his country, was going to kill probably for the first time. They stopped near a police station and waited. Four policemen came out, obviously coming off duty. They rolled the car window down and the lad fired, flooring one of the policemen. The car roared off but there was an army lorry in the side road they had meant to turn into, so they had to drive on at full speed. Dennis glanced at the speedometer; ninety-five miles an hour. Suddenly, a police car pulled out in front. Red tried to swerve around it but hit a wall on the other side of the road. Dennis heard a scream—but didn't know it was himself. And then darkness.

All three of them were dead, the car almost flattened. When the car was searched, several guns were found hidden under the spare wheel. The young lad was still holding another one. Dennis was the only one with identification. A letter from his mother was found in his pocket.

Chapter 11

Rosie was preparing breakfast the following morning. She had had a restless night and had woken up several times. She had a headache, so she swallowed a couple of aspirin and stood stirring a saucepan of porridge. Sean came into the kitchen. He picked up the kettle and made a pot of tea. 'Are you alright, Mam?' he asked. 'Yes I'm OK. I've a bit of a headache, but I've just taken a couple of tablets. I'll be alright when I've had my tea.'

A sharp knock on the door startled them. Rosie opened it and two Gardai stood there. 'Can I help you?' Rosie wondered what they wanted. 'Can we come in, Mrs Connolly?' They followed her in. Sean was pouring out the tea. He offered them tea, but they said no. Rosie sat. 'We've bad news, Mrs Connolly. When did you last see your son Dennis?' 'Last week,' Rosie said. 'He works in Dublin, but he came home for a week and he went back on Saturday. Is he ill?' 'I'm afraid he's dead,' she was told. *'How?'* 'It was a car accident in Armagh.' 'Armagh!' Rosie exclaimed. 'He works in Dublin, miles away from Armagh.' 'He was in a car with two other men. They had just shot a policeman and crashed when they were trying to get away.'

Rosie went very pale, and was trembling. Sean moved over to her and held her in his arms. 'The policeman?' he asked. 'Is he dead too?' 'He is very ill. The bullet just caught his shoulder, but he hit his head on the wall as he fell.' 'Did Dennis fire the shot?' Sean asked. 'We think it was one of the others, the one who was still clutching a gun.'

'Where did Dennis work in Dublin?' Sean told them,' B. J. Williams, the exporters. The Gardai looked at each other. 'Isn't that the place that was raided a while back?' one of them asked. 'That's right,' Sean said, 'about seven months ago.' 'Did Dennis mention any of his friends or workmates?' 'No,' Rosie said. 'Only his landlady and her daughter and he didn't talk much about them.' 'Did you know he was a member of the Provos?' she was asked. 'No, I didn't know. As a family we have never approved of violence. Dennis was going to be a priest, but ran away to Dublin. We had a note to say he was well and we heard nothing more for over a year. Then he wrote and told us he was working and I have written to him several times. Then he came home and stayed a week and went back on Saturday.' 'Weren't you worried about him, not knowing where he was?' one of the Garda asked. Rosie started crying. 'Of course I was worried! I prayed for a letter or a card or something.'

Sean got up. 'I think my mother should be left alone now. None of us knew anything about Dennis or what he was doing. My sisters are waking up and we will have to tell them. I think you ought to leave now and we can talk again.'

The Gardai left, and the girls came in ready for school. 'Who was talking?' Maura asked. Sean told them that Dennis had had an accident. He was dead and the Gardai had come to tell them. He didn't tell them where, or about the guns. They would hear it later. 'Do we have to go to school?' Nuala asked. 'No,' Rosie said, 'we will all have a day off.' Sean said, 'I will go and tell Mr Wilson, and there will have to be arrangements made. I will go to the Garda barracks and find out when the funeral will be. I may have to identify the body.'

Sean was questioned again by the Gardai. 'Did you ever suspect that Dennis was a Provo?' 'No.' Sean was firm. 'Dennis and I were never close. I was always close to my father we worked together. Dennis was always studying. We slept in the same room but he never talked very much. He was secretive. You never knew what he was thinking. We had very little in common.' 'Are you sorry he's dead?' he was asked. Sean didn't answer for a minute. Then he said, 'Well, knowing what I know now, I would rather he was dead than in the Maze Prison for the rest of his life. At least he can do no harm now, and we can get on with our lives.'

Chapter 12

Sean went and told the parish priest and then got on his bike and went to see the Wests. Bob was shocked. Barbara said, 'Poor Rosie, as if she hasn't had enough trouble.' But Liz had always thought that Dennis was a bad one, and she and Sean had often talked about him. At least now he couldn't bring trouble home.

The funeral was three days later. The town's people were divided. Some said he was a hero and had died for his country. Others thought he was a right young fool. There was a photo of Red in the papers. No one had claimed him. The young lad was from Fermanagh and was taken home to be buried. Finally, Red was buried in Armagh. It turned out that he was from Armagh but had been living in the South for years. His elderly sister paid for his funeral. So ended Dennis's short career in the IRA. A young life and a good wasted brain. He had achieved nothing, and if he had lived he would have been told to kill again and again until the memory of the little curly-headed boy had been erased from his mind.

Gareth Nesbitt heard from Barbara West about Dennis's death. He felt so sorry for Rosie. He had never been attracted to women, but he had a great respect for Rosie Connolly. In fact, he almost loved her. She was the nicest woman he had ever met. He loved her children too. They were all quite beautiful, with their shining hair and lovely skin, and so tall and strong looking. He had never came across a family quite like them before.

He decided to go and see them, see if there was anything he could do for them. Just as he was about to get into his car, a young boy rode up on his bike. 'Telegram for Mr Nesbitt,' he called. Gareth took it from him. He opened it and read, 'Your Mother died this morning. Father'.

He would have to go home. His father needed him. He went and saw the Connollys, then bought a ticket at the station for a train to Dublin later that evening.

He put his arms around Rosie and was strangely stirred by her nearness. He put £20 on the table. 'That's your month's rent,' he said. 'I have to go to England for a while. My mother died this morning.' Rosie looked into his face. 'I'm so sorry, Gareth,' she said. 'Were you close to her?' He shook his head. 'No, I haven't been close to either of them, but my father is nearly eighty; he may need me. But I'll be back as soon as I can.' 'Well, take care of yourself and God speed you back soon. We are all very fond of you, and you pay far too much rent for that little house. I feel guilty taking it from you.' 'It's worth every penny to me,' he answered. 'I love it. You must come and see it. The bog is fenced off and the Pass made up. You wouldn't recognise it.' He kissed her cheek and left.

He caught the night boat from Dublin to Holyhead and reached his father's house just after eleven the next morning. His father opened the door and Gareth followed him into the study. The old man pressed the bell by the fireplace. A middle-aged woman came in. 'Doris, this is my son. Could we have some coffee?' She turned and left the room and returned with a tray of coffee and sandwiches. 'I hope you are hungry,' his father said. 'Doris will be hurt if we don't eat them.' They ate in silence for a while. Then his father said, 'How do you earn your living in the wilds of Ireland?' Gareth didn't know how to answer, then said, 'I do a bit of this and that. I live very simply.' 'I thought perhaps that pervert that you lived with all those years had left you some money.' 'Sir Guy left me money.' Gareth wondered where this conversation was leading. 'I knew what was going on, you know,' his father said. 'I never told your mother. She would have been horrified. You never were a man, no games or swimming, no train sets or boxing gloves.' 'I had a very lonely childhood,' Gareth said. 'Only the maid was ever there when I came in from school. I was only happy with Gran. She was always there, cooking and ironing or sitting in her chair knitting or sewing. She was the only mother I had really.'

'Are you living with someone now?' his father asked. 'No,' was the reply. 'I live alone. I am trying to write a book, but I can't always find time to write. I've got to cook and keep the house clean and do the garden. I've got a nice little vegetable garden. I have to do my shopping and washing-up and somehow the day goes so quickly and I find myself ready for bed, and I sleep like a baby. I'm very happy, father. I have nice neighbours and one or two friends. The family I rent the cottage from are a super family. I like them all.'

The entire village attended the funeral. As Mrs Nesbitt had been involved with everything in the place, they all turned out to pay their respects. Mr Nesbitt had arranged with the local hotel to put on a buffet meal and drinks. Gareth caught several people watching him, and saw people whispering. 'Let them talk,' he thought. 'I will soon be back in my little house.'

His father had Doris, who seemed to resent him, but she looked after his father very well. They were company for each other. On the night before Gareth left, his father brought out a small jewellery box. 'This was your grandmother's,' he said. Gareth took it and opened it. There was an engagement ring, a necklace of pearls and a heart-shaped locket. 'I'd rather you took them,' the old man said. 'I don't suppose I will live much longer, and things sometimes disappear when there are no more family.' 'I'll come and see you, father,' Gareth said. 'I'd like that' he replied, 'but I'm very set in my ways and Doris doesn't like visitors. But drop in sometimes.' Gareth wondered what his mother had thought of Doris. Had she ruled the household then, like now—and where had she come from?

Gareth called to see the family doctor. He told him he was uneasy about his father and asked him to call and see him. He told him to send the bill to him. The doctor promised to do this and Gareth began his journey back to County Cavan. He was still uneasy. He couldn't put his finger on the reason, but there was a nagging doubt about the whole set-up. The doctor had just smiled when he said he was worried about his father, but didn't comment.

At the last minute he decided to call at his London apartment and pick out some books, which he arranged to be sent on to him. He found the apartment just as he had left it, spotlessly clean and tidy. He got in touch with the old butler, who hurried in hoping he was going to stay. But he only stayed one night. He passed the time watching the television. He hadn't seen one for nearly two years and he enjoyed it. He telephoned for a meal to be sent in and slept in the four-poster bed, and found himself crying for Guy and for his poor old dad. He hadn't cried for a long time and the tears helped to wash away the loneliness. Next day he travelled back to Ireland, arriving in Belturbet on Sunday afternoon. He had left his car at the Railway Hotel, and as he drove carefully along the Pass he saw Sean and Liz

West sitting on the grass among the flowers, wrapped in each other's arms, kissing as though there were no tomorrow.

Poor children, he thought. If Bob West catches them, there will be trouble. But *he* wouldn't tell. He didn't think they had seen him or heard him, and it could stay that way.

Chapter 13

Maura Connolly sat in the little cafe drinking a milk shake. Ken came in, carried his tea to her table and sat down. 'How are you, Maura?' he said. 'Hello, Ken.' Maura smiled her bright smile. 'I'm fine, how are you?' 'I miss Terry,' he said. 'I wish he hadn't gone to England. He should have finished his education. Why has Caroline left?' Maura stared at him. He obviously didn't know about the baby. Well, she wasn't going to tell him or anyone. 'I don't think she was very serious about getting to Training College,' Maura said at last. 'She liked having a good time.' 'Terry was like that too; it's rather a waste of time if one doesn't make the effort. My parents would be bitterly disappointed if I didn't try,' he remarked.

'My mother would be, too. She is quite bright but never got a chance when she was young, but she works and she's got a good job.' 'What about your father?' Ken questioned. 'He died four years ago. My brother Sean and Mam both work, and I've got two sisters and a little brother. My other brother was killed in a road accident.' Maura wondered why she was talking so much. She didn't usually open up to strangers; but Ken wasn't like a stranger. She had liked him the first day they had met. She wondered what he and Terry had ever had in common, but she and Caroline were opposites and they had got on well.

They walked back together, each to their own classroom. Both were glad they were friends. Maura thought Ken was the nicest boy she had ever met, and Ken thought Maura was beautiful. He hoped to see her often in future.

Chapter 14

Kathleen Connolly sat stitching quietly. Sister Maria Rose had told her that if she wanted to get into the fashion trade she would need a few samples of her work as well as her folder of drawings. She had wondered how she could afford the material for garments, so she walked around a jumble sale one Saturday afternoon and saw a pale blue brocade evening dress, a bit sweat-stained under the arms, but otherwise clean. She bargained and bought it for threepence, and a darker blue satin blouse for twopence. She had sat pondering what she could make and suddenly thought of a gent's waistcoat.

She made a paper pattern from a waistcoat of Sean's and cut it out. She wanted to do it all by hand. So here she was getting it together, and Sister Maria Rose was impressed. She walked with her to the shops and they picked some lovely buttons, twelve in all. They cost one-and-six pence, more than three times what the material had cost. The Sister had warned her to get the buttonholes right. That's what the examiner would be looking at. It was looking good. Rosie hoped she wasn't reaching for the moon. The fashion world was a long way from Belturbet, and Kathleen was only fifteen.

When she finished it, having shown it to the Sister, she folded it carefully in tissue paper and put it away. She had decided to make a child's dress, smocked and embroidered, but she had no money. She talked to Sean, who gave her a pound. She was over the moon. She bought some white silk and smocked and embroidered it with pale yellow, a picot hem with yellow button-hole stitches and a border of little flowers. It had taken over a year to finish both garments and she wondered if it was all in vain. How could she, a small town girl, make any impression on the vast world of fashion?

Gareth called to pay his rent. Kathleen was folding the little dress and wrapping it carefully in tissue paper. 'That's nice,' he said.

'How long did it take to make?' 'Months,' she replied. 'I hope it will help to get me into an art college.' She showed him the waistcoat. 'That is beautiful.' He was genuinely impressed.

'Can I try it on?' She smiled. 'Alright, but be careful, it cost a fortune to make.' Rosie laughed. 'All of five pence.' 'That's right,' Kathleen said, 'but don't forget the buttons.' She explained to Gareth how she had got the material. 'That's smart thinking,' he said.

Rosie, suddenly serious, said, 'I think you ought to do a course at the Tech. You don't know if you will even get into fashion. I'd like you to have a trade to fall back on, if things don't work out.' 'What kind of course?' Kathleen asked. 'What about typing and shorthand, like Liz did? You could start in September and you would still be under eighteen when you finish it.'

Gareth agreed with Rosie. He had known people in the fashion world when he lived with Guy. They were a hard, brittle lot and could crucify a little girl like Kathleen, and she would be working from dawn until midnight. But he intended to get in touch with a few people he thought could help her. Was there no end to this talented family? he wondered. Sean was now manager at the factory. Maura was doing very well at Tech, and now here was Kathleen, with great sewing skills and drawings which were breathtakingly beautiful; and sensible Rosie making them keep their feet firmly on the ground.

He thought about Nuala. She was Rosie's right-hand person, cleaning, ironing and cooking, nearly as well as Rosie; and Patsy the Botticelli cherub. Gareth loved this young boy. At the moment it was football, fishing and bicycles, but it was a young boy's life. Let him enjoy it. Gareth had bought him the bicycle for his ninth birthday and he had started riding out to the cottage and sitting talking, mostly about great football teams. Manchester United was his favourite. Gareth found himself reading about football so he could talk to the boy and pretend to be interested.

'I'll take you over to England and you can watch them play,' he said one day. 'Perhaps for your tenth birthday.' Patsy's great eyes opened wide. 'Would you really!' he gasped. Gareth laughed. 'Yes, really, if that's what you would like.'

Later he wondered if it was a good idea. He was attracted to the child and found himself thinking what it would be like to hug him. He sometimes ruffled the golden curls, but didn't want to frighten the lad.

Chapter 15

Mr Wilson sat down wearily at his desk. Sean looked at him. He was tired and drawn, his eyes bloodshot. 'You need a holiday, sir,' Sean said. Wilson smiled grimly. 'Not a holiday, Sean. I'm retiring. I have sold the factory site. All the business is being transferred to Manchester. There will be some job losses, but the people who have bought the site are opening a large gift store, good stuff, Irish linen, Irish lace, Belleek china, Waterford crystal, as well as cheap little souvenirs, elves, fairies, small stuff for children to buy for their Mams. But you, Sean, I want you to go to Manchester. It's a big job, but you know it, and you are good.' 'Why are you retiring, sir?' Wilson was quiet for a minute, then he said, 'I've felt unwell for a while, so I've seen the doctor, who sent me to a specialist, and the long and short of it is, I've got lung cancer and I want to spend what time I've got left with my wife and children. I've hardly seen them since I opened this place. I love them dearly, but work took over my life. So there it is. The thing is, will you go to Manchester? Your mother will get a job with the new people, but there would be nothing here for you. Sleep on it.'

Sean waited until the girls had gone to bed before he mentioned it to Rosie. 'Manchester?' she said. 'Do you want to leave home? The rent for the cottage and my wages are ample for us to live on. So don't feel bad about that. Maura will be independent in twelve months' time and Kathleen won't stay around for much longer, so it's only Nuala and Patsy.' 'I will always stay in touch Mam, you know that, and I will help you financially if you ever need it. I'd rather like getting out into the world.' 'Liz West won't be happy about it,' Rosie said. 'I know,' Sean said, 'but our friendship will never get anywhere.' Underneath his bravado he felt sad, leaving Liz. He had never looked at another girl. He loved her dearly and he dreaded telling her, but tell her he must.

On Sunday, he rode his bicycle out into the country. The bog was beautiful purple and pink heather and pale green. He walked through the gate and saw Liz sitting in their little garden.

He sat beside her but didn't touch her. 'Is anything wrong, Sean?' she asked. 'I've got to go to work in Manchester.' 'Why?' she cried. 'I know my uncle is closing the factory, but there is something else opening, can't you work there?' He put his arm around her. 'I can't go backwards, Liz. I've got used to management and a good salary. I will get that in Manchester.' 'What shall I do when you are gone?' She started crying. Sean pulled her towards him. He wiped her eyes and kissed her. She clung to him. Her hands stroked the back of neck. His hand touched her breast and she didn't stop him. They touched each other and kissed, and finally they made love. This had happened once before and they had been frightened, but this time they just wanted each other, so in love were they. They lay in the long grass and made love again. They forgot the world and all their troubles.

Liz arrived home several hours later, flushed and tousled. Her mother said, 'Where have you been, Liz?' 'I had a long walk, but it was very windy.' 'Well, it's time we had the milking done.' Barbara didn't go for long useless walks. She couldn't understand her daughter at all. She had seen her on the Pass, putting flowers there several times, and she had missed some plants from the garden. She hoped some young farmer would ask Liz to marry him. She was a great worry.

Liz had other ideas. Several young eligible men had asked her out, some with an eye on her father's farm, and some genuinely liking her for herself but she had always said no.

Chapter 16

Nuala was preparing the evening meal. She loved cooking and had made a casserole with her new potatoes, peas and carrots, followed by apple pie and custard. She had picked up several letters from the mat, glanced at them and put them on the table.

Kathleen came in next. She had taken Rosie's advice and was doing shorthand and typing. Gareth had told her it would be useful to know if she got into the fashion trade, so she was going along quite well.

'There's a couple of letters on the table for you,' Nuala said. Kathleen grabbed them and looked. 'I wonder what these are about?' she said. 'Well,' Nuala laughed, 'you will never know if you don't open them.'

'I've got an interview! Hooray!' 'Where?' Nuala asked. 'Belfast College of Art and Design.' 'Belfast?' Nuala queried. 'Mam will never let you go to Belfast, with all the troubles there.' 'There's troubles everywhere,' was the answer. 'I'm going, if I have to walk all the way.'

'What's all the excitement about?' Rosie came through the door. 'I could hear you half a mile away.' She's got an interview,' Nuala explained, 'in Belfast.' 'I didn't know you had applied to Belfast.' Rosie sounded worried. 'I applied to three places.' Then she remembered about the other letter. It was from Dublin: sorry, there are no more vacancies, but apply next year straight away and make sure of a place.

'Let's have our tea,' Rosie said. 'Where's Patsy?' 'He came in, changed his clothes and went off on his bike. Down to Gareth's again. He nearly lives there. Gareth has promised to take him to watch Manchester United playing and he won't give up till he has been.' 'Girls,' Rosie said as they ate their meal, 'I have work tomorrow. I know I don't normally work on Saturday, but we open on Monday and I have to decorate that big window and, to tell you the truth, I don't know where to start.' 'I'll come and help you,' Kathleen said. 'I'd love to do a nice display.'

When they stopped for a cup of tea, Kathleen and Rosie were thanked, and Kathleen was handed a pay packet with five pounds in it.

'Come and work for us,' she was asked. 'Sorry, I can't,' she answered. 'I will be off soon to art college in Belfast, at least I hope to. I've got an interview on Wednesday. As much as I've enjoyed this morning, I have to go. It's what I've always dreamed of.'

'Well, good luck,' John Brown said. 'Perhaps one day I will be selling the things you make.'

Chapter 17

The shoe factory had closed four weeks ago. Sean had left for Manchester and the house was quiet without him. Rosie missed him. They always walked to work together. The factory had changed beyond recognition, all freshly painted, with several big windows put in, carpets on the floors, and specially locked cabinets for the Waterford crystal and Belleek porcelain.

Kathleen was eager to get to work with Rosie on Saturday mornings. She had great ideas for the display windows.

When they arrived at work, there were piles of material, boxes of crystal, boxes of china, Aran jumpers and Donegal tweed skirts. Kathleen picked up a length of soft green silk and arranged it on the base. A matching length she pleated and spread fanlike across the back, with a length of cream with a pretty shamrock pattern pleated and fanned on the other side. She placed a Belleek tea service on the green side and six crystal wine glasses with two decanters against the patterned material. In the middle she put a life-size model wearing an Aran jumper and Donegal tweed skirt. Rosie watched and wondered if it was enough. It looked lovely, and then she saw the new owner and managers outside looking at it. They were nodding their heads. Rosie went out and joined them.

'Is it enough?' she asked. 'My daughter planned it.' 'It's just right, very effective. We can fill the other window with the cheaper stuff. Yes, Mrs Connolly, I like it. I will tell your daughter.'

The other window was great fun. Little china cottages and churches, fairies and elves peeping around the curtains, and solemn teddy bears with tee-shirts with the national flag; babies' rattles and dolls' tea-sets, little wooden trains and fire engines.

Chapter 18

Liz West waited for a letter from Sean. She was getting panicky. She thought she was pregnant. Gareth came in for his milk and said, 'My typewriter is playing up. Do you know anything about them, Liz?' 'Yes,' she said. 'I'll come and have a look at it this afternoon.' Her mother said, 'We have a busy day, Liz.' 'I won't be long. I expect it is something simple. I'll hurry, I promise.'

When she went up to the cottage, Gareth said, 'The typewriter is OK. I've had a letter from Sean, with one for you enclosed. I couldn't give it to you in case your mother saw.' He handed her the sealed envelope. On the outside was written 'For Liz'. 'I'm afraid your parents would take a dim view if they knew I was aiding and abetting you and Sean,' Gareth said.

'Don't worry about it, you won't have to do it much longer.' Liz was busy reading. 'I'm going to England to him, we will get married as soon as possible.' 'What are you going to tell your parents?' 'I will leave a note. They are going to the Wilsons all day Sunday. I'll have time to get away.' 'What about the milking?' 'The Larkin boys can do it. I'll ask them after Mam and Dad leave. Will you see me to the bus around midday on Sunday?' Gareth hesitated. 'Oh please, Gareth.' 'Alright,' he said at last. 'I hope my head won't roll. They will never forgive me if I help you to leave home.' 'I'll get there somehow, whether you help me or not,' Liz said. She had a handful of £5 notes. Sean had sent her the fare in the letter.

Gareth went to get the milk on Sunday. Barbara said, 'Bob and I are going to the Wilsons.' 'Is Liz going?' Gareth asked. 'No,' was the reply. 'She could come with us, but she won't. I don't know what's the matter with her.'

Chapter 19

Rosie sat round the table with Kathleen, Nuala and Patsy. 'Bob West hasn't been in lately. It must be a fortnight since we've seen him,' Rosie remarked. 'Nor Liz, either,' said Nuala. 'She never missed a week, but I haven't seen her since Sean left.' Rosie gave her a sharp look, 'I think Liz came to see us all,' she said. Kathleen laughed. 'If you believe that, you would believe anything. Any fool could see she worshipped Sean, and he her, but Bob West would rather see her dead than married to Sean.' 'I'm glad he is in England,' Nuala said. 'Perhaps he will meet some nice girl and marry her. He hasn't written for a couple of weeks. I expect he's busy and looking for a flat, although he said the lodgings were comfortable.' 'What's a flat?' asked Patsy. 'It's a floor of a house with a bedroom, kitchen and a bathroom, all on one floor and perhaps a sitting room. He's earning good money now, he can afford a place of his own.' 'I'll have a flat in Belfast when I get to the art college, if I can get someone to share it. It will be cheaper.' Kathleen had got a place at the college and was over the moon. She talked about it incessantly. Nuala thought how peaceful it would be when she was gone.

Nuala was good at school, but not bright, and had no ambitions. She hoped she would meet a nice boy, get married and have a family. In the meantime, she helped her mother, cooked and ironed after school and on Saturday, cleaned the house and polished the furniture, and was entirely happy doing it.

A few days later a letter arrived from Sean—just a note to say that he and Liz were married on Saturday and that he would write later. That evening Rosie opened the door to Bob and Barbara West. They were in shock, both pale and nervous. Rosie said, 'I had this note from Sean. How can he be married to Liz? He's in Manchester.' 'So is Liz. She went off two weeks ago on a Sunday, while we were out. She left a note to say she was going to England. This morning we had a letter to say she's now married to Sean,' Bob said.

Barbara burst out, 'I will never forgive Sean for taking our daughter away. I always thought he was a nice boy. How could he do this to us?'

Rosie turned and faced her. 'Barbara, why are you blaming Sean for all this? Liz is of age, and she has a mind of her own. They have done this together. I had hoped when Sean went to Manchester that she would find someone of her own religion, but I don't mind. If they are both happy, then so be it.' 'How can they be happy when they have hurt us so much?' Barbara was sobbing. 'You and I will have to get used to it,' Rosie declared. 'I don't think they will lose any sleep thinking about us. I am going to send them a card and a present and I'd advise you to do the same. I don't want to estrange them. I love them both, and I will always be here for them, as I will for all my family.'

Bob and Barbara soon left, and Rosie sat thinking about Sean and Liz. She was very sorry the Wests were hurt, but angry that Barbara had blamed Sean. Dear Sean, always helpful and kind. Rosie missed him, and she thought Liz could have fared worse. A lot of the young farmers that Barbara wanted her to marry would have only wanted the farm and her money. That was the way Protestants did things—like marry like—and money marry money. Well, Liz had fooled them all, and Rosie hoped that Sean would love her and take care of her, which was all Liz ever wanted.

Chapter 20

Gareth took Patsy to Manchester to see the team play. They visited Sean and Liz, who were beaming with happiness and with Liz showing signs of pregnancy. Gareth left Patsy with them and went to see his father. The old man was vague and his speech was slow. Doris wasn't pleased to see Gareth. He called the doctor and was told it was senile dementia, but he was well looked after and Doris was devoted to him. He called on the family lawyer and was surprised to hear that his father had signed the house and its contents over to Doris. The lawyer explained that the old man had done it a week after Gareth's mother had died. 'I'm sorry,' he said, 'it should have come to you after his death, but although I tried to talk him out of it, he insisted.' Gareth wasn't worried. He had no very happy memories of the place and had more money than he could ever spend, as well as a lovely apartment in London.

When they got back to Belturbet, Gareth took Patsy home. Rosie was more interested in Sean and Liz than in the football match. Patsy said, 'Liz has got fat.' Rosie looked at Gareth and he nodded. Well, that explained a lot. 'What's the flat like?' she asked. 'It's lovely,' said Patsy. 'They have even got a television set, and Liz is a good cook. We had our dinner there last night and Sean loves his job. They have asked me over for a holiday.' 'We will have to wait and see about that,' Rosie said.

Rosie went to the churchyard every Saturday and tended Dennis's and Hughie's graves. She had put a stone on each. She sat down on the grass and tried to sort out her life.

On Friday, she had gone out with the owner of the shop in his car to order and buy goods. Rosie knew the lines that were selling and she advised him. On the way home he said, 'You could do the buying, Rosie. You know how to sell and you know how to buy.' 'I can't drive a car,' Rosie objected, 'and if I could, I could never afford one.' 'Well, what if I paid for driving lessons and you could use the company car?' Rosie was silent for a while. 'I've got two children still at school, give me time to talk to them,' she said at last.

She had talked it over with Nuala and Patsy and they were all for it. 'You'll get more pay for that,' Nuala said, 'any maybe you could have a car of your own sometime, and you could teach me to drive when I'm old enough.' Patsy was most enthusiastic. Then he said, 'Gareth will probably teach me anyway.' 'You mustn't keep bothering Gareth,' Rosie said. 'He'll never get that book written if you keep dropping in all the time.' 'He's always glad to see me,' was the reply.

Chapter 21

Nuala was busy in the little kitchen. Maura was coming home for the summer recess and Kathleen was coming home from Belfast. Nuala was making sure there was plenty of food ready. The three girls hadn't met up for months. There would be plenty to talk about.

Rosie came in from work and came and put her arms around Nuala. 'The house looks lovely and you have cooked all this. Where would I be without you?' Nuala kissed her cheek. 'I love cooking and the housework is a dawdle. Sometimes I wish I was clever like Maura and Kathleen, but I really love doing what I do, but I expect after September I will have to earn a living. But I won't leave you, Mam. Not yet anyway.'

Rosie watched her with loving eyes. She wondered how long before she, too, wanted to get out into the world. This dear child had never caused her a moment's anxiety. She often lay awake wondering what Kathleen and Maura were doing, and Sean with a family now. 'Perhaps you could go to Technical College and learn cooking, what do you think? The others all went there, but you don't have to.'

'I think I'd like that,' Nuala said. 'I wonder what Patsy will do. He's nearly twelve. All he wants to do is fish and play football and talk to Gareth. Gareth spoils him, and it's not good for him.' The girls arrived home starving hungry and full of chatter. Maura at twenty was nearly six feet tall, with long slender legs, and she walked like a queen with her shoulder-length, swinging, shiny dark hair. Kathleen was an inch or two shorter. Her fair curly hair was cut fashionably short and she had a beautiful complexion. 'Are these my two little girls?' Rosie looked at them in wonder.

They sat over the dinner table, talking. 'Sean's little boy will be over a year old soon,' Rosie said. 'He promised some photos. I'd love to see them all.' 'Why don't you take a week off and go over there?' Maura said. 'Have you had a holiday since you started work?' 'No,' was the reply. 'But I think I will go. We are not busy, but I've a driving test in two weeks. After that, I'll arrange it.' 'I can't believe it,' Kathleen laughed. 'My Mam driving a car, and you don't look like a Granny at all. Fancy you sharing a grandson with Barbara West.' 'Have they forgiven Liz for marrying Sean?' Maura asked. 'I doubt it,' Rosie said, 'but at least they are keeping in touch. I think calling the little lad Hugh was the last straw, but it was Liz who insisted. Sean was pleased, but I'm sure the Wests are furious. Well that's his name. They will get used to it and I'm sure he is a lovely baby.'

Rosie passed her driving test with the same attitude that she did everything. She was nervous the first time she drove the car alone, but after the first day she drove happily. She asked for a week's holiday before the Christmas rush and booked a flight from Dublin to Manchester. She would have liked to take Nuala, but decided it was better to leave her at home to keep an eye on Patsy.

Sean and Liz were delighted to see her and she was fussed over by all their friends. She babysat and let them have a night out, and they gave a party for her on her last evening. She could now put her mind at rest. They were still in love and had no money worries. Liz was a good thrifty housekeeper and they were saving to put a deposit on a house. 'You are not coming back to Ireland then?' she asked. They both said no. Sean explained, 'Here no one worries what religion we are. I go to church with Liz and sometimes she comes to church with me. The baby was christened in my church but he can please himself when he's older. A lot of people here don't have their children christened at all, but we couldn't do that. He will attend both churches as he grows up and make his own choice.' 'I could never see that happening in Ireland,' Rosie said. 'But it makes sense. There are a lot of different religions in the world, and a lot of stairways to Heaven.'

Chapter 22

Rosie arrived back loaded with presents. She forced herself to go and see Bob and Barbara West. They were very surprised when she drove herself up to their house. She brought photos of little Hugh and a letter from Liz. Barbara thawed out as she looked at the pictures of her grandson. 'Are they happy, Rosie?' she asked. 'Very happy, but why don't you go over and see for yourself? They would love to see you and Bob.' 'We can't be away together.' 'Nonsense! The twins are quite capable, and Mrs Larkin would run things for you for a week.'

Barbara looked at Bob. 'What do you think, Bob?' she asked. 'I think we should go. Robert could take a week off and see to things and, as Rosie says, Mrs Larkin would see to the house and I'd love to see my grandson.'

Rosie came home happy. It would be nice for Liz to see her parents. Maura sat at the kitchen table, drinking tea with a young man. 'Mam,' she said, 'This is Ken. We met at Tech and we have kept in touch. Ken is learning engineering.' Rosie liked the open freckled face. He had grown up a lot since his days in the Tech. They walked down the path holding hands. Well, thought Rosie, it had to happen sooner or later. A series of giggles brought Rosie back. She tiptoed to the bedroom. Kathleen and Nuala were peeping through the curtains at Maura and Ken.

'Have you met Ken, Mam?' 'Yes,' said Rosie. 'He seems a nice young man—and what are you wearing, Nuala?' Nuala looked down at her black velvet shorts. 'Kathleen gave me these. She made them. Aren't they super?' On the bed was a pile of clothes, all the colours of the rainbow. 'There's a dance in the Town Hall tonight, and we are going.' 'Who's we?' Rosie had always made the decisions about where her children went. 'Me and Nuala. Ken's going home to change and he's picking Maura up. It's alright, isn't it?' Nuala asked anxiously. 'I can only go when the girls are at home, and it's going to be a great night.' 'Don't go off with some boy then, and you're not going in those shorts.' The girls fell about laughing. 'Of course we're not wearing shorts to a dance! I've made lots of dresses. We are going to take the Town Hall by storm.' Kathleen hugged her mother. 'I will take care of Nuala and I'm used to going to dances. We go several times a week in Belfast.'

Maura came in and Rosie left the three of them trying on dresses. She made a cup of tea, and after an hour of arguments and giggling, the girls were ready. Rosie felt so proud of them, all different but somehow a little alike. Patsy looked up from his comic and gave a wolf whistle. Rosie swiped him with the newspaper. 'Where did you learn to do that?' she asked.

Three bleary-eyed girls got out of bed very late next morning. Rosie had got the day off. She made tea and toast as they told her all about the dance. 'Did you enjoy it, Nuala?' 'It was great, I never missed a dance. My feet will never be the same again.' 'And,' said Kathleen, 'she danced most of the time with Kevin McCaulay.' 'Do I know him?' Rosie asked. 'Sure you do, his parents own the Railway Hotel.' 'You mean little Kevin? He's only a child!' 'He's seventeen and a half years old, Mam. He was a year ahead of me in school. He's a great dancer.' Nuala was hugging herself and looking dreamy.

'Did you dance every dance, Kathleen?' Rosie asked. 'Most of them,' Kathleen replied. 'It was a great night altogether.' 'And Maura danced all night with Ken, I suppose,' Rosie said. 'Yes,' giggled Kathleen, 'and he gazed into her eyes all the time.'

Rosie didn't know whether to be glad or sorry. It looked liked she was losing her hold on her family. At least they are telling me what they are doing, she thought and that's more than a lot of Mothers get.

As she walked down her back garden, a blackbird was singing its heart out. There had been a blackbird's nest in the thorn hedge every year. Rosie climbed the bank and peeped into the empty nest. 'How can it be so happy, when all its children have left?' she thought miserably. Perhaps it was wiser than she was, and perhaps the young ones came back to visit, just as her children would always come back to see her. And she still had Patsy.

Kevin McCaulay began coming to the house and Nuala would stand talking to him at the gate. They went to the pictures together a couple of times, then Nuala told Rosie she was going to tea with the McCaulays on Sunday.

On Sunday night, Nuala came in and announced to Rosie and Patsy that she had been offered a job at the Hotel. 'What doing?' Rosie asked. 'Helping the cook, and I can go to Tech one day each week for City and Guilds.' Rosie was pleased. The McCaulays were a nice family. Kevin helped his father, but couldn't serve in the bar yet until he was eighteen, though he helped stock up and do the cleaning.

They were pleasantly surprised what a good cook Nuala was. She had turned sixteen, but she was very mature for her age and after six months at the Tech she had a mock exam and got an excellent report.

At Christmas there was a party at the Hotel after the bar closed. All the Connollys were invited and a great time was had by all. Mrs McCaulay sat in a corner with Rosie and said how pleased they were with Nuala. She confessed that they had been afraid Kevin would want to go away to work, but he was happy to be at home now and she thought it was because Nuala was there. Rosie said she was glad at least one of her children was happy to stay at home. So, by and large, things were working out well for everyone.

Kathleen told Rosie that she felt she was wasting her time at the art college. She was going to finish the course and then she and her flatmate Ilish had applied to work in a fashion house in London. If they got the jobs, they were going to ask Gareth if he knew where they could find a flat. Maura came home at Easter and showed them a lovely sapphire and diamond ring. She and Ken had got engaged, but didn't plan to marry for a couple of years. She was going to start teaching in September, at a rather select private school at Bray, near Dublin. Ken had a job as maintenance man at a factory. They were saving for a house.

Chapter 23

Gareth Nesbitt was depressed. His book was almost a non- starter. He had torn up all he had done, and had then stared at the blank paper for weeks, but couldn't put a word down. So he put the typewriter away and worked in his garden. He kept thinking of Patsy Connolly. He thought of him all day and dreamt of him at night. He sat at the table trying to do the crossword in the *Independent,* but wasn't getting very far when Patsy came in. 'What are you doing?' Patsy asked. 'Trying to do the crossword,' was the reply. Patsy came and stood beside him. He put his arm around Gareth's shoulder and looked at the puzzle—six across, Inspector Morse's side-kick. 'That's Lewis. I watched that at Sean and Liz's place.' Gareth was shaking and could hardly write. 'Are you alright?' Patsy asked. 'Yes, yes, I'm fine. Let's go and wash the car.' Armed with two buckets of soapy water, they started work.

'Telegram for Nesbitt,' called a voice and the little lad from the Post Office rode up on his bike. Gareth opened the yellow envelope. 'Your father died this morning': it was signed by the solicitors. Gareth hurried indoors and started throwing clothes into a case. 'I'll drive to Dublin and fly over. I'll leave the car in the long stay car park,' he said. 'How long will you be gone?' Patsy asked. 'Two or three days, no more.' He put his case in the boot and turned to find Patsy crying. 'I wish I could come with you,' he sobbed. Gareth gathered him into his arms. 'I will have to go, Patsy. I'll be back soon, I promise.' Patsy stood wiping his eyes as Gareth drove away. Gareth had left the key of the door with him and told him to take whatever food there was to Rosie, as it would go off.

He sat down in Gareth's big armchair and cried. He loved Gareth so much. He took salad, bread, milk and butter and put it all in a bag, locked up and started off home. Thank goodness Rosie wouldn't be home for a few hours. He didn't want her to see he had been crying.

He felt a bit ashamed about his feelings for Gareth. So he swilled his face with cold water, got out his fishing rod and went and sat on the river bank. The fish weren't biting and he didn't try very hard, but he caught a couple of grey bream and went home. Rosie had just come home. 'What's this food in the carrier bag?' she asked. 'Gareth's had to go home. His father died. He said to use it or throw it away. He didn't want it to go off in the heat.'

'Poor Gareth,' Rosie said. 'Now he has lost both parents. He doesn't seem to have many relations. I wonder will he stay in England now. He will probably get his father's house and money. He may not come back.' Patsy felt gutted, then said, 'He'll have to come back for his car, it's in the long stay car park, and all his lovely books. He won't leave them. The cottage is really nice, Mam. You should come out and see it.'

Rosie hadn't been up to the cottage since Hughie's funeral. She always meant to go, but kept putting it off. 'We'll go there in the car after tea,' she said. 'It's time I looked at my property, such as it is.'

She drove carefully up the Pass. Spying the flowers at the side, she stopped the car and got out. Dahlias and gladioli bloomed in a riot of colours. 'Who did this?' she asked. 'I think Liz started it and Sean helped her. Gareth has kept it tidy since they went away.' 'They never said a word about it,' Rosie said. It was a lovely thought. She stood for a few minutes deep in thought then got into the car and drove to the door of the cottage.

Patsy unlocked it and she stood and stared. It looked so homely, but nice and clean. Gareth was a good tenant. She walked through the rooms and into the garden. Potatoes ready for digging, cabbages, carrots and broad beans just drying off. The roses on the wall tied up neatly, everything in good order.

They locked up and went to the Wests to tell them Gareth was away. They had had their holiday with Liz and Sean and were satisfied that Liz was happy. Bob had offered them the deposit on a house, but Sean had said, 'Thank you, but we can do it. If we get stuck we will ask, but we would like to manage it ourselves.' So Barbara now knew that Sean hadn't married Liz for her money. Barbara made tea and sandwiches and they sat and talked like old times. Mrs Larkin came in every day for a few hours. She was glad to earn a few shillings and was a good worker. The twins were growing up too and, though great practical jokers, they worked hard and gave no trouble.

Gareth caught the Shuttle and was in Heathrow by nine o'clock. He caught a train to Eastbrooke and went to the solicitor's home. He was greeted warmly, and when he said he would get a bed at the pub the solicitor wouldn't hear of it. 'You can stay here, dear boy,' he said. 'Your father and I were old friends. We will go to the funeral together tomorrow, but there is business to sort out in the morning.'

They went to the office early. Gareth's father had set up a trust for him many years ago and the solicitor explained that there wasn't much money. He suggested that Gareth pay for the funeral expenses. Doris was demanding to know where all the money was, and the solicitors thought she had been drawing money out of the bank, thinking there was plenty. Gareth was surprised about the trust and was happy to agree to paying for the funeral.

Doris glared at him during the service. She had a rough-looking man with her. Gareth shook hands with them both and was glad when it was over. He never wanted to go back there again, so he went to his apartment in London. Old Potts, the butler, had kept it well, not a spot of dust anywhere and there were fresh flowers in the hall and on the dining room table.

He looked through his telephone book and found a couple of estate agents that he and Guy knew. He rang and asked about flats to rent or buy. He wanted Kathleen in a decent district when she came to England. If he couldn't find one to rent, he had decided to buy one and to let it to Kathleen at a rent she could afford. He thought it was the least he could do for Rosie and her family. He had so much money and they had to fight for every penny, and they were such good people. He had thought of letting her and her friend use his apartment, but he wanted to keep that apart. It was Guy's home and now his, and young girls could mess it up. He liked it the way it was, peaceful and quiet.

Both estate agents had flats to sell and Gareth decided to stay a few days and look at them. He found what he wanted, a second floor flat, two bedrooms, living room, kitchen and shower room. It was sparsely furnished, but he decided to leave it. They would add what they wanted. It was a fifteen-minute bus ride to the City centre and it was terribly expensive, but it was money invested. He had a feeling that after a couple of years they would be off again, probably to America. Kathleen had all the signs of a high flyer.

Altogether it took ten days to get the flat and he found his trust fund very healthy. He met with a few old friends and looked into the bookshop where he used to work. It hadn't changed much. He bought a few books to take back, most of them for Patsy who he had found liked reading. History seemed his main interest.

He drove back from Dublin, stopping on the way to buy bread, cheese, bacon and eggs. He would manage on that until tomorrow when he went into Belturbet to tell Patsy he was home.

Patsy was pathetically pleased to see him. 'I thought you had changed your mind,' he said. 'About what?' Gareth asked. 'About coming back,' Patsy said. 'You've got a lovely place in London which I would die for. I don't know why you live here at all.' 'My true friends are here,' Gareth said. 'I love your whole family, but especially you, Patsy.'

Patsy hugged him. 'When I'm old enough, I'd like to live in London with you—for a little while anyway.' 'When you are old enough, I'll take you around the world. But don't tell your Mam, she would throw me out of the cottage.' 'I guess she would at that,' Patsy laughed. 'Only one and a half years to go and I will be finished school.' 'Have you ever thought what you will do when you finish school?' Gareth asked. 'No, not really. I'm not mad about hard work. I'd like to work in a bookshop or something like that.' Gareth told Kathleen about the flat. He didn't tell her he owned it. She and Ilish had been over to London and were accepted at a fashion house. They both knew it was going to be very hard work and that it would be some time before their drawings would be used.

Kathleen started in the sewing room, sewing sequins on a wedding gown. Ilish was in the cutting room, most of the time sweeping up the bits and keeping it tidy, and being screamed at by the Head Cutter, a nasty little Frenchman who waved the scissors at her. Everyone else just ignored him, so Ilish learned to do the same.

After a year, a couple of Kathleen's drawings were used and turned out very well. They were used in the summer collection and the models were enchanted with them. The orders poured in and Ilish thought her turn would never come, but six months later a Harris tweed cape and skirt she had designed was used and they both felt they were on their way.

Their salary improved after that, but Kathleen thought they weren't paid enough. She resented her ideas being turned into hard cash for the bosses.

At home she was working on Maura's wedding dress. 'Not too many frills and flounces,' Maura said. 'I'm better in plain styles.'

The sitting room of their flat was covered with patterns and material, so they shoved their two single beds into one room and used the other bedroom as a workroom.

'We could start our own boutique,' Ilish said, in fun. Kathleen looked at her. 'You are right, Ilish,' she said, 'and then what we sell would be our own.' 'If they find out, we will be sacked.' Ilish wasn't sure, but Kathleen said, 'We will use our own patterns and buy our own material, and to hell with them.' 'Where will we find customers?' 'We will think of something. If we make enough money, we can stop working for them.' 'Could they take us to court, do you think?' Ilish was nervous. 'I don't know. I'll write to Gareth and see if he can find out where we stand. Let's keep our heads down until we hear from Gareth.'

Gareth read Kathleen's letter. He had thought of coming to London with Patsy. Now he decided to ask Rosie if Patsy could come with him. His lawyer would be able to find out the legal rights of the two girls.

Patsy had finished at school. Rosie tried to find out what he wanted to do with his life, but he didn't say much, just mentioned there was no great hurry. Rosie lost her temper. 'Sean was supporting us all when he was a year older than you. You can't lie around and go fishing all the time. In a few years I will be retiring. Where's the money for housekeeping going to come from? My savings won't last long feeding two of us!'

Patsy got on his bike and went to see Gareth. He told him what Rosie had said. 'She's right you know, Patsy,' Gareth said. 'You mustn't drift around. I'm going to London on business. Come with me. Maybe you will find a job you like over there.'

'You don't work,' Patsy said. Gareth waited a minute before answering. 'I'm lucky enough to have enough money to manage without working, but you will need new clothes as you grow and you can't expect your mother to work for you. Grow up, Patsy, for God's sake! You are behaving like a five-year-old.'

Patsy was on the verge of tears. It was the first time Gareth had criticised him and it had shaken him.

However, Gareth was soon back to his old cheerful, easy-going self, and Rosie said Patsy could go to England. She gave him money for new clothes and insisted on paying his fare.

Patsy loved the apartment, the large rooms and central heating, the television and all the tapes and records. The old butler had made up the spare room bed and, after going out to dinner, Gareth said goodnight to him and went to his room. After midnight, Gareth woke to find Patsy in the four-poster with him. 'I didn't like the strange room,' he said. Gareth just put his arms around him, and the old four-poster saw the beginning of a new relationship.

The next day, Gareth found a job for Patsy in a record shop. The pay was very small, but Kathleen would be coming around and it was better she found him working. She was a smart girl and would have soon guessed at the relationship.

Gareth's lawyer had told Kathleen to make clothes for friends, but to be careful not to take any clients from the salon. They would lose their jobs and probably be barred from other fashion houses.

Maura had a lovely wedding. Sean and Liz came home for the occasion. Kathleen and Ilish brought home the dress and the bridesmaids' dresses. Kathleen was in pale green and Nuala was in apricot. Rosie was bursting with pride as she walked with Barbara West, with little Hugh between them. Sean, tall and broad, gave Maura away.

Nuala and Kevin announced their engagement. Gareth and Patsy arrived looking splendid, and Rosie watched them all with love.

Gareth had decided to go back to London to live. Of course Patsy went with him.

Rosie thought, 'Soon I will be alone, but Nuala will be living nearby and Maura and Ken will have a car and be down quite often.'

Little Hugh loved the Wests' farm. He wanted to stay with his grandparents, so Sean and Liz had to promise to come over again soon. Bob hoped young Hugh would take over the farm when he was older. It was nice having a child about the house, and Liz was pregnant again. Robert was working in Africa with a team of doctors, helping refugees.

Rosie put her tired feet on the footstool. It was rather nice to have the house to herself at last.

The Connolly Connection

Chapter 1

The sun shone mistily through the green blinds on the kitchen window, as Gareth Nesbitt retrieved his boiled egg from the cooker. At last I am going to do something positive, he thought.

Six months ago, he had been almost suicidal. Patrick had been behaving abominably. He had arrived home after being out nearly all night and brought two young men with him, all three high on drink or drugs. They made breakfast for themselves, throwing food around the kitchen and breaking dishes, and then went out again leaving the mess behind.

Gareth was trying to clean it up when Margaret arrived; he had never seen her lose her temper before.

When the kitchen was back to normal she made coffee and said, 'Gareth, when is it going to stop?—you are letting Patrick get the upper hand. Soon he will be taking the pictures off of the wall and selling them to buy drugs for his friends, and they will all be living here—but I'm afraid I won't be coming in, much as I love this place. I could never clean up behind those dirty louts.'

'What can I do?'

'You go and see Mr Langham, he is your closest friend, isn't he? —or you could go to church.'

'Church? I haven't been to church for years.'

'Well perhaps it's time you did.'

Gareth looked at her intently for a couple of seconds.

'Do you go to church Margaret?' he asked.

'Yes, I've been this morning'

'Do you find it helps?'

'Yes. At times I wonder if I'm doing the right thing, but it nearly always makes sense in the end.'

The following Sunday, Gareth followed the congregation into the Roman Catholic Church. He felt strangely at peace as the service continued and when he shook hands with the young priest afterwards.

Since then he had attended every Sunday and had become friendly with the priest, Father Finley by name, 'But call me Tom,' he told him with a smile.

They had sat down to supper in the priest's rather bare rooms, bread and cheese and pickle, washed down with a bottle of beer divided into two glasses. Afterwards they talked and the priest drew him out until the whole story was told—to Gareth's amazement Tom wasn't shocked.

The priest sat quietly for a few seconds.

'There is an Abbey near Oaks in Kent,' he said. 'It's a retreat really, you would get counselling. I could arrange it for you, it's a very peaceful place. I stayed there after college—I was a little unsure that I had the right attitude. I stayed for a month and came away with a clear head.'

Gareth looked doubtful. 'What would I do with Patrick? He would wreck the place if he was left on his own.'

'Perhaps your solicitor would move in for a week or two—you have a good housekeeper, she might look after them both. Patrick couldn't do much with them watching him.'

David Langham agreed rather reluctantly. He didn't like Patrick very much, but for his friend he was willing to make the sacrifice.

So it came to pass that Gareth moved into the quiet Abbey and grew to love the peacefulness. He read the books that he was given— he knew he wouldn't join the order, but he could spend the rest of his life here if he wanted to, and he decided he would do just that—and he couldn't wait to tell David his plans. They were close friends and had known each other since they were teenagers.

David listened gravely, and waited for him to finish.

'But why, Gareth? You are still young, why stay in the Abbey? I didn't know you had religious feelings. Can't you attend church and help them? There is so much you could do and still maintain your lifestyle.'

Gareth shook his head—'I can't go on living in my present lifestyle,' he said. 'I've been blind to my sins, my faults if you like. I would like you to help me dispose of certain things. I want Kathleen Connolly to have this apartment—she will take care of it and she is a worker, it will be nice for her at the end of her busy day.'

'What about Patrick?'

'Oh Patsy! I think I will give him Kathleen's little flat. He won't like it, but he doesn't much care about things. I have arranged an allowance for him. I'm afraid I have spoiled him—'anything for a quiet life,' has been my motto. I have also arranged an allowance for Rosie Connolly—she's retired now and could do with a bit extra.'

Chapter 2

The relationship between Gareth and Sir Guy had been tranquil—their love and respect for each other was always there. Their interest in books and old furniture was mutual, and though they sometimes disagreed about value of things, they never quarrelled.

Patrick was something quite different from the time he found his way into Gareth's bed. He threw tantrums and cried and slammed doors locking himself into the spare bedroom and waiting for Gareth to plead with him to come out, which Gareth generally did and gave him what he wanted.

He had wrecked two new cars in the space of six months, walking away unscathed himself. Since then he hadn't stopped whinging because he wanted another car.

Gareth, nearing sixty, was weary of it all. He was a rich man, but he wanted a peaceful life. Not necessarily an idle life. He was healthy and fit, but he was constantly being torn between keeping Patrick happy and trying to stop him wasting money. Patrick had a good allowance, which he spent like water from a leaking bucket.

So after much weighing the pros and cons, Gareth got counselling from a Monk who heard all about his life and advised him to go home and think it over once more.

And here he was dividing up his assets. First thing, he had to get Kathleen and Patrick into the solicitor's office and explain things to them.

At last a date was found that suited everyone. Kathleen was the first to arrive, wearing skin-tight jeans and a huge white sweater, her natural blonde hair gathered into a bundle on top of her head, not a trace of make-up on her flawless skin. She dropped into a chair with an easy grace.

'What is all this about?' She looked at Gareth, 'Are you giving me notice to leave the flat?'

'Not exactly,' Gareth smiled at her. 'Wait until Patrick gets here and David will tell you everything.'

Ten minutes late, Patrick strolled in, wearing a deep pink velvet suit, a grey silk shirt and tie, his blonde curls hanging to his shoulders.

Kathleen winced as she looked at him—he is so bloody obvious, she thought.

'You are late, Patrick,' David said.

'Late for what?' Patrick asked.

'Just wait please,' Gareth said.

Then David began, 'Gareth has decided to change his lifestyle and this will affect both of your lives. The flat you live in, Kathleen, we suggest Patrick takes over. The rates, water rates and electricity will be paid through the bank, but the telephone you must pay yourself out of your allowance, which will remain unchanged. Kathleen will take over Gareth's apartment. It will be near her work and she needs the space.'

'Gareth are you sure about this,' Kathleen said. 'Where are you going? Where will you live?'

'I will be fine,' Gareth said. Kathleen's concern touched him.

Patrick bounced out of his chair. 'Why have I got to live in the poxy flat?'

Kathleen blushed. 'It's not a poxy flat—I've made it very comfortable and Gareth is putting a roof over your head. But why am I getting the apartment? Can I afford the rent?'

David handed her a package. She looked at it, the deeds to the apartment; it was in her name. 'Why?' she whispered.

'Because you love beautiful things, you will care for it like I have and one of these days you will marry and bring up your children there. That's what it needs, a normal family at last.'

David reached over and gave Kathleen the keys to the apartment and Gareth kissed her cheek.

Patrick remained in his chair when they left. He couldn't believe what was happening—his mind was churning, there was a way out of this, but he couldn't grasp it.

'David, I am going to the newspapers. I will tell all about Gareth and Sir Guy, and how he enticed me into our relationship.'

'Stop!' said David. 'We thought you would try something like this. Well do it Patsy. Your allowance ends from this moment, and the flat will go to the housing market. You haven't a place to lay your head and I doubt if you have a penny in your pocket. Where Gareth is going it won't affect him at all. Don't throw it all away.'

Patrick arrived at the apartment and found Gareth and Kathleen sitting over a tray of tea. He refused to join them and started to pack his belongings.

Kathleen joined him leaning against the door post. 'I've got a taxi —can I give you a lift with your stuff?'

He wanted to tell her to go to hell, but he didn't have the price of the taxi. If Gareth wasn't such a tight arse he would have had a car.

'Thank you,' he said.

When they got to the flat, Kathleen put his cases in the spare bedroom. She showed him the kitchen well stocked with food of every kind.

'I will leave all this for you of course, the food and furniture. I didn't ask Gareth to do what he did, but we should both be grateful to him. Where would we both be without him?'

Patrick's sulky face was red. 'You make a lot of money with your fancy clothes, now you have a fancy apartment you have nothing to complain about.'

'Patsy, listen to yourself. You have never attempted to earn your living, you came as I do from a working class background, so why don't you find work? There must be something you can do. And be advised, get out of pink clothes and try to dress like a man. You look ridiculous as you are.' She paused. 'Anyhow, I'm going to invite Mammy over for a holiday. I hope you'll be able to explain to her how you have been living—and she won't appreciate the pink suit.'

Chapter 3

Rose had picked up the letter from the mat and smiled as she recognised Kathleen's handwriting—Kathleen's letters were always a joy to read. She talked of just getting back from Hong Kong or New York as though they were down the road.

But as she read this letter she frowned. Where was dear Gareth going? And Kathleen having the nice apartment while Patsy was just having the flat.

She had never come to terms with Patsy living in Gareth's house and his strange clothes—and he was so handsome but never had a girlfriend. Could he be one of those men that liked other men? She jumped up and started her housework—what a horrible thought. Living alone is making me fanciful, she chided herself.

Now she had the opportunity to go over to London and stay with Kathleen. She would see Patsy and would go to Manchester and see Sean and Liz. Perhaps stay a few days with them and enjoy the grandchildren.

Sean and Liz brought the children over to Ireland every summer, but Hugh wanted to spend his two weeks in the West's—the hay making, milking the cows, the chickens and turkeys were his chief topic of conversation for months after the holiday was over.

Carol was happy with Rosie and they usually wandered through the little town of Belturbet, stopping for coffee and ice cream or going into Cavan and buying clothes. Carol loved clothes shops. Is she following in Kathleen's footsteps? Rosie wondered. At ten years old she had very definite ideas about what to wear and what suited her.

Rosie sighed. Perhaps she would take her down to London and see Kathleen's wonderful boutique, so beautiful and so expensive.

Where did the English ladies find so much money to spend on clothes?

The following morning another letter dropped on Rosie's mat, a long envelope, thick creamy paper and the name of a firm of solicitor's from London.

She read about Gareth entering the Monastery and leaving her an allowance of a hundred pounds per month for life, and thanking her for her kindness to him while he lived in her cottage.

So that explained why Kathleen had got the apartment and Patsy the flat, but what had driven Gareth to take such a step?

She sighed—perhaps she would never know.

Chapter 4

Kathleen was waiting for Rosie at Heathrow. She hugged her and told her quite truthfully that she looked younger than ever—her plain black suit, white with a red bow tie and high-heeled court shoes, made her look taller than her 5ft 2 inches.

'I've ordered myself a car now,' she said as she hailed a taxi. 'I've got a place to park it. There was no place at the flat.'

'Has Patsy got a car?' Rosie asked.

'Not at the moment—he's a bit hard on cars.'

'What does he do for a living?'

Kathleen dreaded this moment.

'I don't really know,' she replied. 'He applied for work on a newspaper, but I haven't heard if he got it. I don't see much of him to be honest—I lead a very hectic life. I rang him today, but he wasn't in. I'll ring again when I get home.'

Then to change the subject,' 'Mam, it's a treat to see you I had forgotten how lovely you are.'

'Get away with you,' Rosie laughed. 'You're the lovely one. How do you keep your skin so perfect living in the city?'

'Ah, using the right bottles night and morning, and I don't smoke and only drink a little socially. I have to keep a level head running a business.'

Back at the apartment, Margaret had laid up tea and sandwiches and a cake. As soon as they sat down, she arrived with a silver tea pot and water jug.

Kathleen performed the introductions,' 'Margaret this is my mother Mrs Connolly—mother this is Margaret the daughter of the couple who looked after Sir Guy, and lately Gareth.'

Rosie looked into two steady brown eyes, rosy cheeked and slightly stocky. They smiled and Rosie said, 'glad to meet you Margaret. This tea is just what I need, thank you.'

'You are very welcome Mrs Connolly, hope you enjoy your stay.'

When Margaret left the room, Rosie said, 'Can you afford paid help?'

'Yes—and I'm lucky to have her. She's a great cook, and whenever I come home day or night I find food in the fridge and milk and bread. There is always a meal I can get ready in minutes.'

Kathleen showed her mother over the apartment—she had removed the four-poster and replaced it with a king-sized bed—then she tried to ring Patsy, but still no answer. Perhaps later, she thought.

I'll take you to work with me tomorrow. I'm in the middle of preparing the trousseau for a wealthy family whose eldest daughter has found a husband, at last. Rosie glanced at Kathleen and wondered why she sounded so bitter.

'Is she very ugly?'

'Not very ugly, just very plain and no charm either.'

'What's the bridegroom like?'

'A handsome man, sadly in need of the money his bride will bring with her. It's not a great start, but they'll work it out.'

Next day Rosie sat quietly while Kathleen supervised the fitting. She's right, she thought, she is plain and wooden, not a smile. The mother, on the other hand, was a nice-looking women.

'Is the train too long?' Kathleen asked her. 'We can lift it an inch or two.'

The mother smiled. 'No my dear, it's perfect—you've done well. Now, the bridesmaids?'

'They are almost finished, bring them in anytime. Come, I'll show them to you,' and she ushered her into another room.

Oh's and Ah's could be heard, then the mother emerged.

'Darling, they are lovely—come and see.'

The daughter walked slowly after her mother. 'Yes, very nice,' she murmured.

Chapter 5

Kathleen had attended a party with Gareth and Patrick about a year ago. She had looked into the eyes of Robin Delaney, and was lost. They'd talked and danced and then met again and again.

He was heir to a crumbling old house in Hertfordshire; most of the land had been sold off. His father and grandfather had gambled away a large fortune and Robin tried to scratch a living letting out fishing and organising shoots. He loved Kathleen dearly, but couldn't marry her. He needed big money to clear his debts and put his house in order.

Kathleen was deeply hurt and refused to see him again. He tried to keep in touch but she wouldn't take his calls. To her horror she found herself pregnant, and with heart rending tears streaming down her face at unexpected moments—dearly wanting to keep his child, but knowing it was impossible, she slipped off quietly to a clinic and had an abortion, thinking it would end there. But she felt cheated, ill used and bereft.

Her staff were worried about her. She worked on and finally came to terms with it, until three months ago when she was asked to dress the bride for her wedding with Robin Delaney. Rosie didn't know all of this and would have been horrified—abortion was a crime against God. Kathleen truly believed this too, and she still had nightmares about it, but how ironic, out of all the fashion houses in London, they picked Kathleen Connolly.

Next day Kathleen was gone all day. Rosie picked up a book and read it for a while, Margaret came in and cleaned the apartment and cooked lunch. Rosie, idly looking round, saw a key rack; all the keys were labelled and one said 'the flat, 41 Torburry Road.'

'Is this the flat where Kathleen lived?'

'Yes it is—it's a twenty minutes bus ride from here. Mr Patrick lives there now.'

'I think I'll go and see him.'

Margaret looked doubtful. 'Perhaps Kathleen will take you there this evening.'

'No,' said Rosie, 'I will find my own way, if I get lost I'll call a taxi.'

Rosie found the right bus, the key to the flat safely in her handbag. Perhaps I'll tidy up for him and make him a meal, she thought. She found the road and the number, climbed the stairs, put the key in and turned it. It was very quiet. He must be out, she thought.

What a mess in the kitchen, crumbs all over the tops and flies in the butter. A lump of cheese looked cracked and hard. She walked through the small lounge; bottles and cans littered the coffee table. She tripped on a pair of trousers. Picking them up, she put them across a chair and walked to one of the bedroom doors.

There, she almost screamed aloud. On the grubby bed lay Patsy, his limbs entwined with the limbs of a bigger man. The man was slightly coloured, and they were both fast asleep.

She tiptoed from the flat and called a cab from the kiosk on the corner.

Numb with shock, she let herself into the apartment, took her coat off and lay down on the bed. She crawled under the eiderdown as she shivered. Margaret had heard her come in, she gently opened the door.

'I've made you a cup of tea.'

She gazed at Rosie's ashen face, and sat down at the edge of the bed. Rosie looked at her.

'You knew and tried to warn me, didn't you.'

Margaret nodded. 'It's a terrible shock for you.'

'How long have you known?' Rosie wanted to know.

'Every man who has lived here for years has been like that, Sir Guy, Gareth and Patrick.'

'Why did you stay?'

'They are still people who need looking after. It's sad for them, hiding their feelings from the world, never having children of their own. Mostly they are gentle people, very kind and polite. Patrick was spoiled by Gareth, he was given everything he wanted and got selfish and sometimes he lost his temper. I don't think I could have stayed if he had got the apartment. He frightened me sometimes, but Kathleen I could die for, she is a credit to you.'

Rosie was silent. 'Would you like an aspirin with your tea?' continued Margaret. 'If you have a little nap you will feel better. Don't blame Kathleen for not telling you—I think she hoped you would never find out. She lives for you and was trying to shield you.'

Rosie sat up, sipped her tea and swallowed a couple of aspirins.

'Are you married?' she asked Margaret.

'Yes my husband is the caretaker of these apartments. He repairs leaking taps, mends doorbells and moves furniture around if needed. We have two children, my daughter Sarah is a SRN at Guys hospital and my son James is at Manchester University.'

'Good children then,' Rosie said.

'Yes,' Margaret replied. 'By the grace of God we have been lucky.'

Rosie held Margaret's hand. 'You deserve to be lucky. I was thinking terrible thoughts about Patsy, but you have given me the other side, and I agree it must be a lonely life and a lonely old age— like poor Gareth, wealthy but he still has nothing.'

Chapter 6

Kathleen parked her new car in the mews behind her house. All the old stables had been turned into garages. She ran up the back steps which led into the kitchen.

'Where's mother?'

Margaret looked at her for a moment. 'Sit down please, Kathleen. Your mother saw the key to 42 Torbury Road on the rack and she decided to go and see Patrick. I tried to talk her out of it but she caught a bus, and arrived back in a taxi looking like she'd seen a ghost. She's lying down in her room.'

Kathleen's face was a mask. 'Do you know what happened?'

'No she didn't tell me, but she knows about Patrick. I tried to help her to see both sides, but she has had a shock, no doubt about that.'

Kathleen found her mother sitting at her dressing table, brushing her hair.

'Your hair is lovely, mam,' she said instinctively, 'so thick and shiny.' Then softly, 'I've spoken to Margaret and she told me you've had a shock. I'd hoped you would never find out. How are you?'

Kathleen hugged her, and Rosie gave a wistful smile.

'I certainly was shocked, but I decided it is nothing I can put right, so I will enjoy my holiday. If Patsy comes to see me I will not make a scene as much as I'd like to—it's no good blaming anyone.

'At first I was furious with Gareth, but it must have been there all the time and Gareth brought it out—as would someone else sooner or later. Patsy is beautiful, but not very masculine.'

She broke down and sobbed as Kathleen held her. 'What would your father have said to all this?'

Kathleen grinned. 'He would have had a shock if he'd seen any one of us. Look at Sean, a managing director, Maura, a head teacher, me, a high flyer going places poor dad never heard of.'

Rosie wiped her eyes and said sadly, 'And Dennis died an outlaw and Patsy a queer, what a family'—then, 'a bit like most families I'd say.'

'A bit more good than bad,' said Kathleen. 'Come Mam, put your glad rags on—we're going out to dinner in a posh restaurant.'

They walked the half a mile to where a table was booked. As they examined the menu, Kathleen looked up. Patrick had entered with a tall, swarthy, but very handsome man, and was fussing around him as they took their seats at the table.

Kathleen watched them over the top of her menu. Patrick seemed besotted with the other man. Suddenly he looked over and saw them. Rising in surprise, he came over and kissed Rosie's cheek, which she rubbed hastily with a napkin.

'You look well, mother.'

'So do you,' she replied. 'Are you alone?'

'No, I've got a friend with me. I'll bring him over in a minute.'

When they had finished the meal, Patrick introduced them.

'This is Charles—my mother and my sister.'

Charlie shook hands with Rosie, admiration in his dark eyes. Then he took Kathleen's hand and kissed it. She withdrew it as quickly as she could.

They chatted for a while and drank coffee. Charles was a well-educated man, but Patrick paid for the meal and the extra coffee.

Patrick was anxious to get away—he noticed how Kathleen had affected Charles and was bitterly jealous, but was afraid to make a scene. He would have if it had been Gareth, but Patrick was learning fast. Charles would have hit him or walked away for good, either was unthinkable.

Charles was English. He was the illegitimate child of an Italian mother and an English father. His wealthy father had paid for his upbringing and he was educated at a good school where he just missed being expelled for stealing. When he was eighteen his mother had died. His father got him a job in a bank, but he wasn't happy and left. He'd lost touch with his father and had lived on his wits for about ten years. He gambled when he could afford it, he played cards and usually won, but he found it cheaper go with boys like Patrick. It kept a roof over his head—but he liked the look of Kathleen. It was a pity she was Patrick's sister and she was smart enough to guess what as going on.

pity she was Patrick's sister and she was smart enough to guess what as going on.

96

Chapter 7

Rosie caught a train to Manchester. Sean and Liz were delighted to see her. She stayed a week, and young Hugh said he would like to go back to Ireland with her. He was fourteen years old, tall for his age and broad in the shoulders.

'Go on Dad, let me go. School has broken up for six weeks, and I can be of help to granddad—he's getting old now.'

'Don't let him hear you say that,' Sean said, 'he thinks he's 23.'

'Well he's nearer 70!' Rosie said. 'He doesn't do as much as he used to, but the Larkin twins are still there.'

'I wonder why neither of them are married,' Liz said. 'They were really nice looking lads.'

'The poor girl who married one of them would have to marry both, unless she had a twin,' Sean laughed. 'Even then she would still get them mixed.'

'You can go home with mother,' Sean told Hugh. 'We will be going over to Ireland in a month's time and you can come back with us.'

'I don't know why I have to come back here, Dad,' Hugh grumbled. 'I love it on the farm—I could go to college over there.'

Elizabeth and Sean looked at each other; they had been hearing this from Hugh every time Ireland was mentioned. They would have to give it some serious thought, Sean decided.

Chapter 8

Ted Armstrong had begun his working life as a builder up in the East End of London having left school at 14 years of age. He was quick and streetwise from when he was nine years old.

He got called up in 1939 when war broke out; the army life suited him. He was a Staff Sergeant when war was over and he came out with £100 and a ready-made suit of clothes. He looked around at war-torn London and guessed that builders would be needed, bought a second-hand pick-up truck for £50 and went touting for work. He soon had plenty. He priced fairly and found a few friends who wanted work to get started.

In a very few years he had built a thriving business. He never skimped on work and he kept his prices fair. He was a hard boss; he wouldn't tolerate bad work or bad time keeping.

In 1958 he was knighted Sir Edward Armstrong. He had married the daughter of an impoverished family who rather looked down on him, but he really loved his wife and she him. Sadly he had no sons, but three daughters who mixed with the elite of London Society.

The eldest daughter Ruth had suffered with acne as a teenager and her mousy straight hair and large mouth made her shy, but she had a lovely slim figure and quiet brown eyes, and the friends that took the trouble to know her realised what a lovely person she was.

The whole family went to Ascot, where she met Robin Delaney. She fell in love with him there and then. He paid attention to both her and her two sisters, laughing and joking with them all.

Sir Edward asked him to join them for lunch, and Robin's charm won them over. Rachel, the second daughter, was very pretty and vivacious and poor Ruth stood quietly by worshipping this delightful man, but in the end it was Ruth he had asked to come for a car ride in to the country the following day.

They drove to his home in Sussex, where his old housekeeper had prepared lunch, and as they sat in the garden Robin decided to ask her to marry him at some time in the future. They met quite frequently for another month before he popped the question. She was delighted and said 'yes' at once, but as she reached to kiss him, she found he kissed her gently but without passion. She felt slightly hurt at this, but decided he was just holding back.

The parents were overjoyed. A wedding day was set, and Sir Edward and Robin had a meeting in the study where a settlement was arranged.

Ruth would have preferred it if he had told her he loved her, for although he was kind and attentive at all times and no one could find fault in him, he never said those very important three little words.

Robin was having dinner at the Armstrong home when Rachel said, 'Robin, wait till you see Ruth's wedding dress, it is absolutely beautiful. Kathleen Connolly is a wizard.'

Robin choked on his mouthful of food, and excused himself by saying something had gone down the wrong way. The ladies fussed over him and poured him some water, but Sir Edward, always sharp, wondered if Kathleen's name had been the cause. He knew in his heart that Robin needed Ruth's fortune, and he hoped that he loved her.

He carried on with his meal, but pondered in his heart.

Chapter 9

Rosie and young Hugh arrived back in London having persuaded Sean and Liz to let him come to Ireland with her. Hugh was a cock-a-hoop; granddad's farm was the only place he wanted to be.

Patrick had walked in to Kathleen's workroom wanting to know where Rosie was. Kathleen told him she was in Manchester but was coming home the next day.

'You could have told me she was here,' he grumbled.

'I rang you three times, and you were never there—then she got the key and let herself into your flat, and came home looking like a zombie. She knows you're gay.'

'I'll take her out to dinner and the Theatre.' Patrick wondered how to face his mother. He hoped she wouldn't make a scene in the restaurant.

'Yes, do that,' Kathleen said, 'and don't bring Charles, if you can bear to be parted.'

'God you are hard, Kath—you have all this and a lovely home, but you don't care a damn about me.'

Kathleen didn't want a scene. She knew anything she said would be useless. As soon as mother and Hugh were gone, she would tell Margaret to keep him out of the apartment and she would put the phone down when he rang. She did not like his gay friends, who would only desert him when he was short of money.

Patrick called for Rosie and they went off for the evening. Kathleen was teaching Hugh to play chess when the doorbell rang. She opened the door to find Charles on the step.

'Hello,' he said. 'As Patrick has taken his mother out, I thought you could do with the company.'

'My nephew is staying with me, and when he goes to bed I've got book work to do,' she replied. 'I've been neglecting it since mother got here.'

Charles had hoped to find Kathleen on her own. She was beautiful and had a good business. He could see a future for himself with her, but Kathleen could see through him. The nasty little money-grabber, she thought. Rude though it seemed, she didn't want him in her home and she couldn't imagine what they would talk about. She shut the door and went back to Hugh.

'Who was that?' he asked.

'He's a friend of Patrick's,' she said. 'I don't like him much—I didn't ask him in.'

Next day Rosie and Hugh left for home. Patrick came round to say goodbye—he had a black eye and a cut lip.

Rosie was horrified. 'Whatever happened to you?'

'I was mugged last night on the way home,' he lied.

Kathleen knew what had happened. Charles had been in a foul temper. When Patrick came home having spent all his money, he had lashed out; and as usual, Patrick had taken the burnt of his anger.

He looked so sad and pathetic, Kathleen was almost sorry for him, but there was nothing they could do. She hoped that Charles would soon move on, but she knew that before long there would be someone else.

'Did you call the police?' Rosie asked.

'No, there was no point—they were long gone with my wallet and my watch.

Rosie produced £50 out of her bag. 'Take this,' she said, 'it will help you out'

Patrick took the money and thanked her. Kathleen was livid. Thank God mother was going home, and she wouldn't need to see this miserable wretch again.

'Look after him,' Rosie whispered as she kissed Kathleen goodbye. Kathleen didn't answer. She wouldn't make promises she couldn't keep. They got in to the taxi and were gone.

Kathleen looked at Patrick. 'You lying little toad,' she yelled. 'Charles gave you a hiding, didn't he? He came around here last night, but I didn't let him in. I'd advise you to do the same or you will end up on the mortuary slab next time.'

Patrick turned and left. He had £50. He would pay Charles and all would be well again.

Chapter 10

Kathleen worked hard trying keeping her mind occupied, trying not to think of Robin's wedding looming nearer each day. She had given her best; the wedding gown was perfect, as were the bridesmaids' dresses. She was delivering them herself to make sure they arrived as perfect as could be, and she didn't contemplate running into Robin as he spent his days in the country.

The dresses were carried reverently up the wide staircase by Kathleen and the two bridesmaids. Lady Armstrong watched from the hall, smiling as Kathleen came down.

'The tea trolley has just gone in,' she said. 'Please come and join us.'

Kathleen followed her reluctantly into the drawing room. Ruth, Rachel and sixteen-year-old Jane sat waiting for their mother to pour.

'How did you learn to sew so beautifully?' Rachel asked.

'I was educated at a Covent,' Kathleen answered. 'I really started sketching before I started sewing. I used to draw these really outrageous gowns and colour them in, and then I won a sewing competition with a brocade waistcoat and a baby's dress. After that my mother bought me a sewing machine, I attended the School of Art and Design in Belfast, and then came with a friend to London. My friend got married and I carried on, on my own. I love what I do.'

'Perhaps you'll make baby gowns for Ruth,' young Jane said, 'when she gets a baby of course.'

'Maybe,' Kathleen said, then rose to go.

She really hadn't thought of Robin and Ruth's children, and her eyes misted over remembering the child she'd had taken away. She hurriedly said goodbye and left, finding it hard to drive with tears streaming down her face.

Will this haunt me forever? she asked herself. God forgive me.

One week to go until the wedding, a very grand affair of 500 guests. Kathleen was paid £8,000 for her work, her biggest cheque yet. The gown was a masterpiece of fine art, and she expected the orders would be coming in after the wedding, so she looked for extra workers.

It was hard to get women who knew how to do the bead work and such fine stitching, but she managed to find two people, a couple of middle aged sisters, and she was well pleased. Both of them had been ladies maids, both were single, they lived together and were glad to earn a bit of extra money.

The wedding day arrived at last. Kathleen slipped on her warm robe and stood by her window. It was 6.30 am and the beginning of a fine day—the early morning dew sparkled on the lawn and a few autumnal cobwebs glistening on the shrubs. Was Robin thinking of her or Ruth? She thought the poor girl looked unhappy, but she was getting the best man in the world. She ought to be deliriously happy.

Ruth was glad the day had arrived at last. She wished it wasn't going to be such a grand affair, but it was only one day long. Robin had never mentioned love; he kissed her with the same passion as if she was his grandmother. She was going to spend her life with a stranger, a stranger who she loved desperately but couldn't get close to.

A housemaid brought her breakfast—a lovely tray with a pink rose in a crystal vase, orange juice, toast and marmalade and coffee, lovely scalding hot coffee. Then she bathed and came back to find a cosmetic lady waiting to make her face up. Then the hairdresser did wonders with her mousy hair—she hardly recognised herself. Her mother fussed in and out all the time, at last helping her into her beautiful dress. She stood in front of the mirror and her heart lifted— she looked really good. Robin would tell her he loved her—yes, he would tell her today.

Her smile was radiant as she walked slowly down the stairs. Lady Armstrong had left with the bridesmaids, and her proud father waited for her at the bottom of the stairs. A servant handed her a sweet smelling bouquet, they got into the Rolls and were smoothly driven away to the church.

Chapter 11

Patrick was having a bad time learning to do his housekeeping, and Charles was no help. When Patrick had money, Charles wanted to eat out all the time, and when the money ran out, Charles disappeared for days arriving back bad tempered and sometimes abusive.

One night as Patrick sat in front of his television, the phone rang. It was a pleasant male voice,' 'Is that Patrick? I'm a friend of Charles.'

'He isn't here,' replied Patrick.

'Can I come round for a chat?'

'Why not? I could do with a bit of company.'

'I'll be there in about 20 minutes,' said the voice, and hung up.

Patrick put the phone down slowly. It was an educated voice, and he wondered what he wanted. Well, I'll soon find out, he thought.

He opened the door to a tall man, Patrick guessed in his early forties. He slipped off his overcoat—underneath he wore a dinner jacket and a black bow tie. Putting a bottle down on the coffee table he looked around for glasses. Patrick fetched them from the kitchen and sat down on the couch.

The man sat beside him and poured out the drinks. 'Cheers Patrick.'

They talked about things in general. He told Patrick his name was Robert, and he kept filling the glasses. After a while he got up and walked into the bedroom—Patrick followed him, wondering what he was doing. Robert had undressed and lay on the bed

'Come and sit here Patrick.' Smiling, he pulled Patrick down beside him.

An hour later he got up and dressed. 'Thank you Patrick,' he said softly, kissed his cheek and then left.

Patrick was in shock; he got up and walked into the lounge. There was fifty pounds in notes on the coffee table.

Charles came back the next morning. 'Let's go out to dinner tonight,' he said affably. 'You have money now, haven't you?'

Patrick nodded. He didn't know how to deal with the situation and he was frightened of Charles.

About a week later the same thing happened—a different man this time, a rougher man. Patrick didn't like him much. Later as he sat in the lounge, Charles came in and picked up the fifty pounds and put it in his wallet.

'Good lad Patrick,' he said, 'you are sitting on a gold mine.'

'I didn't like him,' said Patrick. 'Why are you doing this?'

'It's good money, he left happy and you are none the worse. I'll make us a cup of coffee.'

After he had put a mug of coffee down in front of Patrick he said, 'I don't understand why you feel bad about it, think what we can do with all that extra money.'

Patrick started to cry. 'I thought you loved me,' he sobbed.

'Darling, of course I love you, you are the greatest and you are beautiful,' Charles held him in his arms. 'Go to bed and get some sleep we will go out tomorrow, we will go to the races.'

Charles sat after Patrick had gone to bed. Here was a nice little earner and he was getting his own back at snotty stuck-up sister Kathleen Connolly. Wouldn't she be mad when she finally heard that her brother was a call boy and, though Patrick didn't realise it, he was going to be very busy in future.

But much as Charles would like Kathleen to know, he hoped she wouldn't hear about it for a long time. When she heard she would definitely do something to stop it, and Charles wasn't ready for that just yet.

Chapter 12

About a year later Kathleen picked up her mail and glanced through it as she walked to the car. A letter from her mother—lovely, she thought. Mam's letters were always full of news from the neighbours and old friends and about the rest of the family. They all kept in touch in a vague way—the odd phone call or a post card—but Mam kept in close touch with them all.

She sat down at her desk with a cup of coffee and opened Rosie's letter. All the usual news, but at the end Rosie wrote,' 'I wish you would go and see Patsy, I had a letter from him and I get a feeling he's in some kind of trouble—he didn't say so, but reading between the lines I feel there is something wrong. I know you disapprove of him, but just for me, Kathleen darling, call in and see him, Please! Please!'

Kathleen thought it's not like Mam to beg, and much as she hated the idea of going round to the flat, she decided to go for Mam's sake.

She went after work that day. Patrick opened the door, wearing a pale blue dressing gown.

'Oh, hello!' he said in surprise. 'I was just off to bed, I've got a sore throat.' He seemed reluctant to let her in, but she forced her way past. 'What brings you here, sister?'

'Mam asked me to—she wondered if you were okay. You are still her baby, even though you're in your twenties.'

They talked trying to find something to talk about. Kathleen got the impression he wanted her to go, so she left, but driving her car to the end of the road, she turned and drove back again, parking a few doors from the flat.

After about fifteen minuets a taxi pulled up, a middle-aged man got out, paid the driver and went into the flat. Kathleen waited. The taxi came back half an hour later, the man came out and it drove away.   Just as she was about to go, Charles came walking up the street and went into the flat.

Next day Kathleen rang David Langham, the solicitor. When she told him what had happened the evening before, he asked her to come with him that night and watch together.

The same thing happened, but two men had called at different times, and Charles had followed them in just like the night before.

Kathleen told David she had to go to Manchester the next day.

'Try to bring Sean back with you,' David advised. 'Tell him what you have seen and between the three of us we will sort Charles out.   I think he's pimping for Patrick and no doubt, keeping the money for himself.'

Kathleen was warmly welcomed by Sean and Liz. After an excellent dinner cooked by Liz and helped by young Carol, Liz excused herself and went to a church meeting.   Hugh and Carol went to bed and at last Kathleen was able to speak to Sean frankly.

Sean was horrified. He had guessed that Patrick was homosexual but had no idea what he was involved in. He agreed to go back with Kathleen the next day, and later asked Liz to ring his work and say that he would be away for a day or two, also warning her that he might be bringing Patrick back with him.

Liz showed some displeasure. She too had her doubts about Patrick. She didn't want him in the house with her children and she said so. Sean who seldom lost his temper snapped at her.

'For God sake Liz, he isn't a criminal, just a silly boy who's got in with the wrong people!'

'It's a long time since he was a boy and God knows what disease he has picked up. I hope you'll have him checked out at the hospital,' she retorted.

Sean was furious. Kathleen tried to calm him down.

'Liz is right, Sean. He has been with a great many people—say you'll get him checked as she asked to put your mind at rest, and make it up with her. Don't leave in the morning under a cloud. You two are the happiest couple I know—stay that way.

Sean and Kathleen got back to London just after mid-day. They had lunch with David Langham and made their plans.

Kathleen and Sean called on Patrick around six-o clock. He was with Charles, but he was pleased to see Sean.

'What are you doing here?' he asked.

'I've been doing a bit of business in London and couldn't go back without seeing you and Kathleen, but I've got a free day tomorrow and I'm hoping you will show me around—Kathleen is too busy.'

Patrick looked at Charles. 'We were going racing tomorrow.'

'Take your brother out, Patrick,' said Charles. 'I can go to the races alone.'

'Are you sure?' Patrick asked.

'Of course I'm sure. We can go racing together another day.'

Sean smiled. 'That will be great, I'm looking forward to a good day out with my little brother.'

Later, when they met David, they couldn't believe their luck. Getting Charles out of the way all day was just what they wanted.

Next day, Sean took a taxi and picked Patrick up at eleven o'clock. Charles had already left, and as soon as Sean and Patrick were gone, David and Kathleen went into the flat. They had found a locksmith to come and change the locks. They stuffed Charles' clothes into bin bags and put them outside the door, and packed Patrick's cloths into suitcases. David took the telephone out of the socket, and informed the police, who knew him well, that Charles might try breaking in when he came back. Then they took Patrick's luggage back to Kathleen's apartment, and warned Margaret not to answer the door in case it was Charles.

Sean and Patrick visited the Royal Mews, Westminster Abbey and then sat in Trafalgar Square.

'Patsy,' said Sean 'I'm taking you back to Manchester with me.'

Patrick looked at him, his eyes full of tears.

'I can't go Sean, Charles gets cross with me, he won't let me go.'

'We know what's been going on,' Sean told him quietly. 'You are not going back to the flat—David Langham has taken over, Charles can't get in, and you and I will be in Manchester before the evening.'

Patrick cried like a baby. 'I don't know how it all started,' he sobbed. 'I thought Charles was like Gareth—he was so gentle, but Charles can be cruel—and suddenly he was sending all these men to me, and when I said I didn't like them he got abusive, so I just carried on. I didn't know what else to do.'

'Well it's over now. Perhaps you should have a holiday with mother, then we will find you something.'

The thought of having Rosie fussing over him, cooking lovely meals and telling him all the news sounded like bliss.

Although Patrick still had a certain beauty, his baby face had lines and his laughing mouth often settled into a hard line—still handsome, but not the pretty boy he used to be. His arms and legs ached and he often felt nauseous. He hoped he would never see Charles or any of his friends again and, much as he had resented Kathleen's good fortune, he knew it was she who had rescued him. Sean had told him all about it. Kathleen had said it was Rosie's letter, but his family had saved him, rallying round as good families do.

A police car was waiting near the flat as Charles walked wearily down the road. He had put his last fiver on the last race and lost it, and he didn't have the taxi fare from the station. He was in a foul mood. That little faggot Patrick had better work hard tonight or he would know why!

He got his keys out and tried to enter, but the key didn't seem to fit. He knocked loudly, but got no answer. He shouted, 'What the fuck is going on, Patrick? Open this door.' Then as he went to put his shoulder to the door, the police came up and asked him what he was doing.

'I live here,' he shouted.

'Not any more.'

'All my clothes and belongings are in there.'

'Your clothes are in those bags.'

Charles looked at the bags in disgust. 'Where is Patrick? He is my friend.'

'I gather he was a better friend to you than you were to him, sir. Now you'd better pick up your things and move on.'

'Where can I go?'

'Would a night in the cells help? I'm sure we can think of something to charge you with.'

'No thank you,' Charles muttered, and started up the road lugging his four bins bags.

Charles looked for a pawnshop, and pawned the gold bracelet which Patrick had given him early in their relationship. He knew it was worth at least £300, but the pawnbroker would only allow him £100. He took it in desperation—he needed somewhere to sleep tonight, and tomorrow he would find another friend. London was full of losers like Patrick.

Chapter 13

Liz gave Patrick a slightly cool welcome, but Hugh and Carol were delighted to see him—they hadn't seen him for years, and they were surprised how quiet he was. They remembered a jolly, light-hearted man and this wasn't at all what they expected—and later that night Liz told Sean she had made an appointment with Dr Frost, their GP. Sean had to admit that Patrick looked ill.

Dr Frost gave him a thorough examination, and rang the hospital, to get an appointment with a specialist that afternoon.

'He must be seriously worried to get him to hospital so quickly,' said Liz.

Patrick went there with Sean, and they decided to keep him in overnight—in fact they told Sean it would be a couple of days. He was put in a side ward by himself, and the specialist told Sean they were testing him for Aids. Liz could be right after all, Sean thought, but where was it all going to end—and how to tell Rosie anther son was in trouble.

The test proved positive, Patrick had full-blown Aids. He was asked to name the men he had been with, but he only knew their Christian names. 'If you can find Charles, he would know them,' he said, but Charles had disappeared.

Sean had to arrange somewhere for Patrick to go. He was still on his feet at the moment. One thing he knew, Liz would never let him back into the house, not with the children. The specialist offered a solution—a hostel for people like Patrick which had a spare room, near Redcar.

Patrick looked gutted. He didn't really feel very ill, but the specialist had talked gently to him, explaining that it would be better not to go home to Rosie. She wouldn't be able to cope when he got very ill, after all she was over sixty.

'My allowance won't pay for the hostel and hospital and everything.'

'Don't worry, Patrick. Your sister is going to rent out your flat, and with the rent and your allowance you should manage. You see, there isn't a hospital in your part of Ireland that could deal with your illness, and they simply couldn't take you. I expect your mother will come and see you, and Sean isn't far away and Kathleen will be up here from time to time.'

Kathleen and David Langham sat down and agreed it was best to let the flat furnished. They changed the telephone number and had a team of cleaners in to clean it up.

'Should we let Gareth know?' Kathleen asked.

David was thoughtful. 'I suppose we had better—he'll be very distressed.'

'We are all very distressed!' Kathleen was angry. Her mother shouldn't have to worry at her age. It was partly Gareth's fault that Patrick was the way he was. Sooner or later it would have happened, but Gareth should feel some guilt—although that didn't make it any easier for the family.

'I ought to write to Mam, but it will be a difficult letter to write. Perhaps I'll go over and tell her—at least I'll be with her. God knows what would happen to her if she reads it and no one's there with her.'

David had to admire Kathleen—a great businesswoman, but soft-hearted where her mother was concerned.

Chapter 14

Kathleen sat on the plane to Dublin, still wondering how she should tell Rosie. How could she break it gently? How would Rosie react?

Arriving in Dublin she suddenly thought, I'll tell Maura first. She rang them and said she was at the airport, she would take a taxi out to Bray.

'You will do no such thing,' Ken told her, 'get yourself a cup of tea—I'll be there in half an hour.'

'Really Ken I can get a taxi.'

'Do as you are told for once, sit down and wait.'

Ken and Maura both arrived..

'Where are the girls?' asked Kathleen.

'Gone on a camping holiday, they left this morning and they'll be back Sunday night.'

'I can't believe they're old enough to go camping.'

'Rozanna is ten and Alison eight, and they're very independent.'

Kathleen smiled. 'I expect that's because their mother is a head teacher.'

'Well,' Maura replied, 'I must admit they have had to rustle up a meal once in a while. We used to, didn't we, and it did us no harm at all.'

Kathleen laughed. 'I could do it better then than I can now. I'm lucky I've got Margaret—she makes sure I don't starve.'

Sitting over supper Kathleen told them the whole story of Patrick. Sheer shock was written on their faces.

'Didn't you know he was like that?' Kathleen asked.

'We thought he might be living with Gareth, but all this other business—how are you going to tell your Mam?'

'I'm hoping you'll come with me and we can tell her together— you will, won't you Maura? I need you with me. I've had a bad week, and poor Sean has had his share. Liz won't see Patrick nor let the children see him either. In fact I'm worried that all this has caused a rift between Sean and Liz.'

'That's her narrow-minded protestant upbringing,' Ken said. 'They're all so smug and self-righteous—I hope the children don't grow up like that.'

'I think not,' Kathleen said. 'To all intents and purposes they're English children, and English people don't worry about which church you attend, if any, so long as you're a good neighbour.'

'Maura you take Kathleen to Belturbet in the morning,' said Ken. 'I won't need the car. The factory's closed until Monday—and don't hurry, I'll be here if the girls get back early.'

'Right then,' said Maura, 'we'll make an early start, about 7.30. We'll call Nuala and she can come with us if she's not too busy. I don't think she does much Saturday lunch time, it's the evenings are her busiest times.'

'She's still doing brisk business then?' Kathleen asked.

'Turning people away most weekends. If you don't book a dinner well in advance you wouldn't get in.'

Ken smiled. 'She gets around that kitchen like a will-o-the-wisp, issuing orders to her staff—I don't know how she keeps them, but they all love her. I suppose that's because she works harder than any of them.'

Kathleen and Maura talked late into the night—they had a lot of catching up to do. Ken went to bed and left them to it.

Maura looked into Kathleen's eyes. 'You are so beautiful, isn't there a man in you life? I can't believe you haven't found someone to love.'

Kathleen was silent for a minute. 'There was one once. He was a lovely man, but he had an old estate, the house needed a lot of repairs, and there were old debts from his father and grandfather. The bank was threatening to foreclose, so he found an heiress and now they're married—and I made her wedding dress.' She was crying now. 'I've never found anyone I could love like I loved him—I think of him every day, and only through working like a slave can I keep going.'

Maura held her and they cried together. At last Maura stood back. 'We deserve a drink,' she said, and got out the whiskey bottle and a couple of glasses.

I'm glad I didn't tell her about the abortion, Kathleen thought, or our tears would have flooded the lounge.

At six o 'clock next morning, Ken got up to make a cup of tea. The whiskey bottle and two glasses were still on the coffee table. He grinned to himself—two sore heads this morning—then he thought, Maura won't be able to drive. He took her up a cup of tea and woke her.

'When did you start drinking whiskey?' he asked.

'I didn't,' she said, 'I tasted it, it was horrible—but Kathleen had a couple. I pretended, I don't think she noticed. She's had a terrible time, and she needed a good sleep.'

'I don't mind you having a drink darling,' Ken said tenderly. 'I was worried about you driving all that way this morning, that's all—but you'll be alright, just take it easy. Better to get there late than not arrive at all.'

He woke Kathleen. She looked groggy.

'Would you like couple of aspirin, love?'

'Yes please, Ken,' she croaked.

'You girls had a bit of a binge in the wee small hours?'

'You could say that' Kathleen replied, 'but it was great having a heart-to-heart with Maura—she's a great listener. I love you all so much, I wish I could see you more often!'

After a breakfast of coffee and toast both felt better, and they got away at eight o'clock.

'This is a lovely part of the world,' Kathleen said. 'You forget how beautiful Ireland is—it's a lovely country alright.'

'If they could stop fighting each other it would be paradise,' Maura answered.

They drove through County Meath with its emerald green fields and lush meadows; fat woolly sheep grazed on the hillsides and sleek cows stood chewing the cud under the trees. Kathleen felt relaxed and rested. All that was left now was facing Rosie and telling her about Patsy, but she had Maura and Nuala with her—they would cope.

Maura drove slowly; the road was in a bad condition, sudden potholes and branches overhanging.

'When we join the EEC, they will allow us money for the roads' Maura said.

'Is there a chance of us joining?'

'Yes, it's all but done. I believe it will make a big difference to the country in general—we're high on the list of priorities.'

At last they were in Cavan. Kathleen glanced at her watch—11.15 am. 'We've made good time considering the speed we had to go—20 minutes now and we will be with Nuala.'

They walked into the bar of railway hotel, and Kevin nearly dropped the glass he was polishing.

'My God, this is great. Nuala was saying just last night how she hadn't seen you for ages—go on into the kitchen.'

Nuala was taking golden apple-pies out of the oven, and the aroma of apples, cloves and cinnamon met them. She yelped with delight, 'Where have you two dropped from? I was telling Kevin last night I never see you, and here you are.' She kissed and hugged both of them. 'Does mama know you're here?'

'No,' Maura replied. 'We're on our way there. Will you come with us? Have you time? You look busy.'

'Call this busy?' Nuala quipped. 'You should see me tonight—we're booked solid from 7 o clock till midnight.'

'How do you keep it up?' Kathleen asked.

'I love it' Nuala said. 'I've got good help, everyone knows the ropes and we all help each other, and at midnight Kevin brings us supper and a drink.'

'Supper?' Kathleen queried.

'A big tray of sandwiches all freshly cut—we couldn't eat cooked food after wallowing in it for five hours.'

They went in to Nuala and Kevin's private sitting room. There they told her about Patsy. She was horrified—she didn't know he was homosexual, she just hadn't thought about it, it was a terrible shock.

'I think we won't tell Mam about all the men,' Maura said. 'She will be worried enough and there's no need for her to know.' They all agreed.

Strangely, Rosie wasn't as shocked as they'd expected. She read a lot, and had read book about Aids and its causes. She said she knew in her heart that it would end this way—what chance had a lad like Patsy in a city like London? 'I hope he hasn't infected anyone else,' she said.

The girls looked at each other—only half of London, thought Kathleen.

'Sean?' Rosie said, 'how is he taking it?'

'He did what had to be done,' Kathleen replied. 'It was hard for him. Liz isn't much help and she refused to see Patsy after he was diagnosed—in fact she dragged his mattress and all the bedclothes down into the garden and burnt them.

'Now she feels safe then,' Rosie said.

'That's it. It's very hard on Sean—the children keep asking what Uncle Patrick has, I think Sean told them it was cancer. Perhaps we should all just say that.'

'Good idea,' Nuala agreed.

Chapter 15

Rosie, Maura and Kathleen walked into town during the afternoon—they wanted to call into the Convent, to see the nuns, who had helped the girls on their way.

Sister Maria Rose, looked old and walked with a stick, and Sister Theresa was Mother Superior. They were so pleased to see Maura and Kathleen.

Sister Maria Rose said she looked through fashion magazines in the newsagents, and if she found Kathleen Connolly's name anywhere she bought the magazine. Kathleen Connolly was her girl, the cleverest and the most beautiful girl in the whole wide world, and Sister Theresa felt the same way about Maura. They all had tea together and Rosie, sitting there listening to them, forgot her troubles for an hour or so.

As they sat round that evening, Rosie said. 'We will go to mass in the morning, the Connolly family united. Nuala and I always sit together, and Tommy.'

'How old is Tommy?' Kathleen asked.

'He's nearly five, a grand lad and very well behaved.'

'And the twins?'

'They've just turned two—a couple of imps, especially the girl Mary—Jack is a bit quieter, but she eggs him on.'

'How on earth does she manage,' Maura asked.

'Kevin's parents don't do much in the hotel—the old man has a vegetable garden. That's where Nuala gets her fresh stuff from, and old Mrs McCaulay has the children with her. Nuala has a young girl to keep her eye on them, but they would rather be over in the bungalow with the grandparents, being spoiled.'

Do I note a hint of jealousy? wondered Maura. Poor Mam. Once she was like the old woman who lived in the shoe, now she rattles around alone. I think I will have the phone put on for her so she can keep in touch more often.

Everyone was up and about early on Sunday. Mass was at nine o'clock and the three Connollys, mother and two daughters, were well worth a second glance. Nuala waited by the church gate. A few heads turned furtively as they took their seats. Maura noticed the Kellys' Connie, her old enemy, had a couple of children with her. She was as fat as her mother was, both were shabby and not very clean. Maura whispered to her mother, 'Who did Connie Kelly marry?'

'Marry?' said Rosie, 'she didn't get married. That's her two eldest—she has another one at home, all different fathers I've been told.'

After mass several people stopped to chat. The Kellys just behind them were heard to say, 'Just look at the swank of them—when they moved to Cavan Road they hadn't a pot to piss in,' and Sister Theresa remarked loudly 'and aren't they a credit to Rosie—I'm as proud of them as she is.'

Nuala asked them to lunch at the hotel.

'You'll have more time to talk, and I'll be cooking anyway. It's not very busy Sunday lunch time, and we don't open the restaurant on Sunday nights—got to take a rest sometime and what better time than Sunday?'

'Thanks Nuala, that will be great. We've got to get back—the girls will be back from camp and they'll need a bath, they always smell terrible after camp, and Kathleen's flight home is eight o'clock tonight.'

'It's a shame you couldn't stay a while longer,' Rosie said.

'Oh Mam, I wish,' Kathleen sighed. 'I've asked Ilish to look in on Saturday in case anything went wrong, but I must be there Monday morning. I've hardly seen my desk for days. I bet there's a pile of work waiting.'

'Dear Ilish,' Rosie said. 'Such a sweet girl—I'm glad you stay in touch.'

'So am I,' Kathleen laughed. 'I've only just finished buying her out. I miss her at work. She was better with the showroom staff than I am. I rant and rave at them—I don't know how they stand me.'

'I don't believe that,' Maura said. 'Bet you're a soft touch if any of them are in trouble.'

They had a wonderful lunch, Roast beef, Yorkshire puddings, roast potatoes and four vegetables. Kevin, Nuala and the children plus Mr and Mrs McCaulay senior sat down with them, and Nuala's young staff waited on them. When the dessert trolley was wheeled in, it was laden with Pavlova, sherry trifle, fresh fruit salad, and hot apple pie with thick cream. Nuala nearly burst with pride.

'I haven't seen better in London,' Kathleen declared. 'No wonder you do good business.'

'Fruit salad for you my boy,' Nuala told Kevin, 'you're getting a paunch.'

'Nonsense,' Kevin retorted, 'I'm still a growing lad.'

'Well you're as big as I want you to be.' Then she said softly, 'You can have a dollop of ice cream on it.' They grinned at each other.

After coffee in the lounge, they all played with the children. Kathleen loved little Mary, her dark hair and eyes like Kevin, she had mischief written all over her face. The little boys were fair like Nuala and the eldest one reminded her of Patsy. Please God let him never go down that road, she prayed silently.

At two thirty, they went back to Rosie's cottage to pick up their overnight bags. Rosie said she would be over to see Patsy—'I'll go as often as I can,' she said.

'You could stay at Sean's.'

Rosie shook her head. 'I will find a bed & breakfast somewhere near Redcar, I think. Liz and I will not see eye to eye. I don't want her to burn my bedding after I've gone.' They all protested. 'Well,' Rosie said, 'I will be sitting with him, touching him, kissing him— you know how Liz thinks.'

Silently they all agreed.

The journey back to Bray was uneventful. They arrived home at six—'just in time for a cup of tea before you go to the airport,' Maura said.

Indoors they found Rozanna and Alison sitting in their dressing gowns watching television, hair still damp and both smelling of roses. The washing machine was burbling around in the kitchen as Ken put the kettle on. Kathleen looked at Maura and said, 'Where on earth did you find a treasure like him?'

Ken smiled. 'There's no more at home. You were right, Maura, they smelt awful so I bathed them and stuck all their dirty washing in the machine.'

'We used nearly all your rose bath salts, Mam,' said Rozanna.

'Well you'll have to buy me some more with your pocket money.'

They both groaned, but Kathleen slipped a coin into each of the two small hands, 'for the bath salts,' she whispered.

Kathleen kissed Maura goodbye and hugged the little girls.

'Come back soon Auntie Kathleen,' they said, 'we hardly ever see you.'

'I will promise.' Kathleen hoped she could keep her word.

Ken took her to the airport and waited until she was ready to leave. He kissed her cheek and said, 'Thank you for being there for Patsy, and your courage telling Maura, Nuala and Rosie. You should have been a man Kath, you are so strong.

Chapter 16

Kathleen leaned back and closed her eyes—another hurdle had been crossed. The family all knew the worst. She would have liked to strangle Patsy for causing so much pain. The family had taken it well, but she knew the sadness it was causing, and it would get worse. The Doctor had told Sean quite bluntly that Patsy would die in perhaps a year or even less, and there wasn't a chance that he would recover.

She dozed for a few minutes, then she was back in Heathrow. When she got back to her apartment Margaret was waiting for her with tea and sympathy. Thank goodness for kind, understanding Margaret nothing shocked her. A long lazy soak in the bath then to bed—and to her surprise she slept soundly all night.

Kathleen was determined to make Charles pay for what he'd done. She had no idea where he was, but she made a vow to herself that somehow, sometime he would be made to pay.

David Langham rang her at work. He told her that he had travelled down to Kent the day before and told Gareth what had happened.

'How did he take it?' Kathleen asked.

'Very badly,' David replied. 'He turned pale, put his head on the table and wept. I felt rather sorry for him.'

'There were a lot of tears shed in Ireland too this weekend,' Kathleen said bitterly, 'and there will be a lot more. Although Mam took it quite calmly. I expected her to pass out or have hysterics, but she said what chance did he ever have in a wicked place like London, and there was no answer to that.' Then after a moment's pause, 'Have the police any news of Charles?'

'They found him on a computer file first as Carlos Benetti, then as Carl Benson and lastly as Charles Ben. They say they want to talk to him—I believe it's about forged cheques or bank cards.'

'I'll look out for him, and I'll see him in prison if it's the last thing I do,' Kathleen declared.

In the meantime, Maura had kept her word. By using a bit of persuasion with the phone company, Rosie had a phone within a week, and loved to talk to her children each night.

She could even ring Patsy—it was good to hear his voice, but it wasn't the joyful bouncy Patsy she used to know; although he said he was very comfortable and had made a few friends, and he always said before he rang off, 'pray for me Mam.'

Patsy was never a great one for praying—it was a day's work getting him to Mass when he was a lad, and she knew he never went to church in London. Nobody goes to church in London, she thought bitterly. All those big beautiful churches half empty on Sunday, while the little church of the Blessed Virgin here at home, could hardly hold the congregation. It's a pity we can't swap them. And then laughed at the thought of St Paul's or Canterbury Cathedral sitting in the middle of Belturbet. They'd have to knock down Reilly's pub and the post office and a few more to get them in.

She was still laughing when the phone rang.

'Hello Mam.' It was Kathleen. 'Are you crying?'

'No,' Rosie confessed, 'I'm laughing', and she explained about having to knock down Reillys pub and the post office and half of main street to get St Paul's in.

Kathleen laughed too. 'You can't do that Mam—where would Connie Kelly pick up her Social and with no pub, where would she spend it?'

'If she's got it!'

Just leave well alone—and seriously, there's usually a good congregation at St Paul's. They're not all really religious, but it's the right place to be seen—all the best people, you know.'

They talked on about many things, and when Kathleen put the phone down she felt happier than she had done in a long time. Mam was coping and she hadn't lost her sense of humour.

And Rosie was thinking, thank God for Kathleen. She is a light in a dark tunnel, and Rosie laughed again thinking what Kathleen had said about Connie Kelly. Then she prayed.

'Dear God, if Patsy has to die, help him through it.'

Chapter 17

Sean wondered if his life would ever be normal ever again. He tried to visit Patsy at least once a week, and Liz couldn't understand why—and long chilly silences followed each visit. She never asked him how Patsy was and she had taken to sleeping in the spare room, and her lame excuse was that she wasn't sleeping very well and didn't want to disturb him.

As he lay wide-awake, he wondered what had happened to their loving comfortable marriage. Would it get better after Patsy died? He didn't realise how much Liz was like her mother. He had always found Barbara humourless and poker faced, all right when things were going her way, but otherwise.... He wondered what a jolly man like Bob West had ever seen in her.

He remembered his father saying that their parents had expected them to marry, so they did. Perhaps Rosie and his sisters had wondered what he had seen in Liz, but he'd been happy enough until now.

Liz too was wondering what had happened to their marriage. For the life of her she couldn't see that it was her own fault. Why on earth did Sean get mixed up in Patsy's sordid affairs in the first place? All she knew was that she wouldn't let Sean touch her after he had been to see Patsy. His sickness disgusted her and she hoped she would never see him again.

Kathleen arrived at work bright and early on Monday morning, but she found all her staff already there. Before she got a chance to say good morning, her assistant manager literally dragged her into the office.

'Oh Kathleen, I really am glad to see you. Three weddings, no less—can we do them, do you think?'

Kathleen picked up the notes on her desk. 'We have to, that's what we are here for. Nine months. We'll get in extra staff. Have you shown them the models?'

'Yes,' Gabby replied, 'two are easy peasy, but the third one is very posh, wants the full works—eight bridesmaids and something special for her Ma. It might be a good idea if you went you see her—I think they were disappointed you weren't here. Anyway, I've taken the liberty of ordering the material for the first two—it will be in this afternoon, so we can make a start.' Then, 'Oh, golly, I forgot to ask how your weekend was?'

'It was nice, having a good gas with my sisters, and all the nephews and nieces.'

Gabby hurried away. Kathleen looked at the three orders—there would be a lot of overtime for everyone for the next nine months, and plenty to keep her busy. Thank goodness for work—she wouldn't have time to think of Robin Delaney.

Kathleen had spent a gruelling three hours with Lady Dunfield and her daughters. She had taken her folder with lots of models—mother wanted one and Alicia wanted another, and they shouted each other down with poor Kathleen sitting waiting for a decision. Mother wanted white, Alicia wanted ivory, and they argued about the style. At last they stopped.

'What do you think, Miss Connolly?' Lady Dunfield asked.

Kathleen smiled. 'I think cream silk and an empire style—the cream would be great with your lovely peach skin and your bright brown curls.'

Alicia nodded. 'Yes, I think you are right.'

Mother nodded too, glad at last to reach a settlement. 'What colour for the bridesmaids?'

Kathleen got in quickly with, 'Pale apricot for the senior girls and a deeper shade a cream for the little ones, apricot sashes and apricot and pale cream embroidery.'

'My head-dress?' Alicia asked.

'Oh I think a coronet of cream roses—silk roses might be best, they will still be fresh at the end of the day. You will look beautiful.'

Alicia leaned forward and hugged Kathleen. 'I'm glad we chose you. By the way, we, my fiancé and I, have decided on an Easter wedding—it gives you a couple of extra months.

Lady Dunfield looked a bit put out. 'I like a really white wedding with pink bridesmaids,' she said wistfully.

'No mother, cream and ivory it is—now what about you? What do you have in mind for yourself?'

Kathleen looked at Lady Dunfield's blue rinsed hair and lovely blue eyes. She knew just the shade of blue, a silk suit with a matching hat, but she said nothing.

'I will think about it and I will come in and look at a few outfits next week.'

The following day Kathleen looked at the other two wedding gowns. 'What is the red chiffon thing?' she asked Gabby. 'That's for one of the brides, red chiffon frills from the waist to the knee and a hat to match.'

'How ghastly!' Kathleen shuddered.

'Actually it will look great on her—she's 5ft 2 inches, and as skinny as a clothes prop, black curls and an elfin face.'

'What flowers is she carrying?'

'A posy of white roses.'

'And what's the groom wearing I wonder?'

'It could be a purple three piece suit in velvet.'

'Ouch!' Kathleen groaned. 'And the other wedding?'

'This is it, a long straight white silk skirt with a split to the knee, and a white silk top to the waist with an embroidered neck line—and she picked this white hat.'

'Ah, that's nice. 'Is she blonde?'

'Yes a natural blonde, shoulder length. She has a great figure, one bridesmaid in pale blue, the same style, and a coronet of little blue roses and forget-me-nots.'

Everything was going well.

When she got home, Kathleen switched on the answer phone.

'Hello Kath, it's Mam. I'm coming over to Redcar next weekend—any hope of seeing you? Maura may be coming with me.'

'Hello Kathleen, David here. Gareth is dead. Ring me when you come in. If you are free I will come over.'

Kathleen slumped into a chair. 'What the hell else can happen?' she thought.

She rang David. 'Come over, I'm in all evening—I haven't the energy to go out.'

She put the percolator on, and put on a silk housecoat and mules. Her feet ached like toothache—she would have a long soak in the bath later.

David arrived and sat down beside her.

'How did Gareth die?' she asked.

'He—he—he....' David was crying. 'He hung himself in the laundry'

'Oh dear God,' Kathleen whispered. 'Did he know about Patsy?'

'Yes, I told him last week.'

'Of course—you told me you'd been down last week. What will happen? Have the police been told?'

'Yes, it couldn't be covered up. He left a note, just the usual—there was nothing to live for, he was sorry to cause so much trouble and to say sorry to Rosie.'

Kathleen poured two cups of coffee. 'Are you hungry David?'

'I don't feel like eating. I could murder a scotch, but I'm driving. The coffee is fine, thank you Kathleen.'

'What will happen about the funeral?'

'I'm afraid the monks are not keen to bury him in the funeral ground. I think cremation is the thing, and leave the ashes in the garden of remembrance. It will be the easiest for everyone—he has no family except your family.'

'And you, David' Kathleen said. 'You were good friends apart from business.'

'Very good friends,' David said sadly. 'He was a very kind gentle person, and he always hated cruelty or brutality. He couldn't hurt a fly. I wish you could forgive him Kathleen—he wasn't to know Patrick would pick up with an animal like Charles, he didn't know people like Charles existed.'

'Mother is coming over next weekend to Redcar. I will see if she will come to the funeral. I can't promise for her—she took Patsy's illness very calmly, just blamed London. Margaret talked to her about Sir Guy and Gareth. I think she accepted what Patsy turned out to be, and of course he is still her baby. He can't remember dad, who was a lovely man, and Gareth was a father figure as well as everything else—and an unending source of money.'

'I think that's what made Gareth retire to the Abbey. Patrick loved spending—he went through nearly £20,000 during the years he spent with Gareth.'

'As much as that?' Kathleen exclaimed. 'How rich was he?'

'No one really knows—I would say over £50 million, and there are shares and houses all over the spare. Guy and Gareth led a good life, but they never wasted money. What they spent is hung on the walls and in the bookshelves, which are now yours Kathleen. Patrick would have sold them if he'd needed money—that's why you got this lovely apartment. Gareth knew you would treasure it. He hoped you would marry and bring up your children here.'

Kathleen gazed at her folded hands and said nothing.

'You've been hurt?' David enquired gently.

Kathleen raised tear-filed eyes. 'You could say that,' she answered.

'Long ago?'

'Nearly three years now.' She wiped her eyes.

'He must have been mad,' David declared.

'It was a question of money,' she said sadly. 'He was in dire straits, old debts, house falling down—we loved each other, but the estate came first and me second. Then he married an heiress, and I made her wedding gown. Ironic wasn't it? She knew nothing about him and me, but she opted for my fashion house, and I had no idea who she was marrying until I delivered the old dress—but it's all in the past now. Perhaps one day I will meet someone.'

'I hope so, Kathleen, I really do.' David patted her hand.

Back in Kathleen's apartment, Rosie asked, 'Where will Patsy be buried?'

'Where would you like him to be buried?' David asked.

'Ideally I would like him buried beside his father and brother.'

'Well we can arrange that, I am sure.'

'Could you really?' Rose's eyes were swimming with tears.

Kathleen hugged her mother, 'Darling, have you been worrying about this?'

'Well yes I have. I just want my men folk all together.'

'How will you do it, David?'

'His body can be flown over to Dublin, be met by a motor hearse there and straight down to Co Cavan. I expect all the family will be in Dublin and follow the hearse.'

'Stop thinking about it, Mrs Connolly. I will arrange everything, and if I can help in any other way in the mean time just let me know.

Patsy died three months later, and David did organise everything. Rosie asked the parish priest to hold Mass, and the church was crowded. Everyone thought he had died of cancer, and one old women in the graveyard said to another, 'he was always delicate looking, and I said to my late husband 'Patsy Connolly will never make old bones.''

The funeral was on Thursday and the family stayed with Rosie until Sunday evening. Sean, Liz and Carol had come over; young Hugh had got his own way and stayed on with Barbara and Bob West after his two-week holiday. Bob West had a mild heart attack and was told to take things easy. Hugh was starting at the agricultural college in Sligo in September. Carol had her way too, and had two deliriously happy weeks with Kathleen in London.

Liz and Sean were polite with each other, and she had to sleep with him in her mother's house or Barbara would have wanted to know why—not that Barbara wanted them in the same bed, but she would hint and probe until she got the truth out of Liz and then she would say, 'I told you so, what did you expect marrying a Fenian.' However, Sean went to stay with Rosie after the first three days and then they went back to Manchester.

It was quiet without Hugh. A healthy sporting lad, he was always in and out of the house, leaving a trail of dirty shirts and socks and football boots. And now the house was clean and tidy all the time and strangely silent.

Carol was a tidy girl. She loved her clothes and always hung them up, and particularly the ones Kathleen had bought for her in London. She had made her mind up—she was going to art college and then to London. She didn't tell her parents as it would cause another argument, and Carol hated it when they argued, but she couldn't wait to get away.

Chapter 18

Rosie and Maura met Kathleen and Sean at Patsy's bedside. Rosie and the girls were shocked at the change in him; Sean who saw him every week had hardly noticed how weak he had become. They had decided not to tell him about Gareth—they couldn't see what could be gained by telling him. Rosie was going back with Kathleen for the funeral. Maura had to get back to her school and Sean didn't want to go—he was having trouble keeping his mind on his work, thinking about Patsy, and the chilly atmosphere at home was getting to him.

Gareth's funeral by Irish standards was a pathetic affair. David, Kathleen, Rosie and Margaret watched the coffin glide away behind the curtains. A priest had said a few prayers for the repose of his soul in Paradise, but did a suicide ever get to paradise? Who knows?

David had all Gareth's affairs in hand, and Margaret and her elderly parents had a substantial amount of money left to them. Kathleen, Rosie and Patrick also benefited, but David put Patsy's on hold, making sure he had every comfort for the rest of his short life and afterwards it would go to Rosie. The Abbey also benefited.

Chapter 19

Kathleen wondered where Charles had disappeared to; she was always on the look-out in restaurants and the Theatre.

She had struck up an acquaintance with Harry Jackson, a single man in an apartment near her; he was very taken with her, admiring her good looks and her business sense. They usually met in the mornings getting their cars out for work, and occasionally in the evenings. He worked for a publishing company. They went to the Theatre now and then and she invited him in for coffee or a drink. He was very reserved and never made any advances, for which she was grateful.

One evening he called and asked her if she would like to go out with him to the launching of a book by a well-known author. When they arrived there were a lot of people drinking cocktails. Harry got them a drink from a passing waiter before being called away. She stood sipping her drink, when a voice behind her said suddenly 'Hello Kathleen.'

She turned, and there stood Robin Delaney. She met his eyes and quickly looked away.

'Hello Robin.' She took a quick drink to hide her confusion, then, met his eyes again. 'How are things with you?'

'Well, seeing you has improved my day.'

She smiled. 'Is Ruth with you?'

'Sadly no. She's gone to the Armstrong villa in Provence with her mother for a while. She hasn't been well—we were expecting a baby and she miscarried. She's very upset.'

I know the feeling well, Kathleen thought. 'I am sorry,' she said, 'but she's still young. Better luck next time.'

'Are you here alone, Kathleen?'

'No, I was invited by my neighbour, Harry Jackson. He works with the publisher. What about you?'

'I came with Rachel, Ruth's sister, and her fiancé.'

'So she's getting married too?'

'Yes. I expect you'll be asked to dress the ladies again, as you did such a wonderful job with our wedding.' Then, after a pause, 'Kathleen will you come out for a meal with me?'

'Do you think that's a good idea? I don't socialise with married men, and really not many singles ones.'

'Just a lunch please,' he said. 'I've missed you so much—I tell you frankly, you were the love of my life. No one could ever take your place.'

'For God's sake, Robin, listen to yourself. You dropped me because I didn't have enough money to bail you out of your debts, and now you tell me you still love me. Where does that leave me? I loved you too, but I've got a life to lead, and some day I will meet a man who loves me for myself not for my business. And strangely, I could at this minute settle all your debts—but it's too late.'

At that moment, Rachel appeared looking radiant—on the arm of Charles.

Kathleen nearly fell through the floor as Rachel introduced him.

'We'll be in to see you as soon as Ruth and mother get back. We're getting married next summer—June I think.'

'I'll do my best for you.' Kathleen forced a smile at both of them, then Harry came back and took her off to meet someone else.

When she got home she rang David Langham.

'David, you will never guess who I ran into tonight. Charles has got himself engaged to Rachel Armstrong, Sir Edward's daughter. What shall we do?'

'I'll ring inspector Duffy—he will be very interested. You don't know where he's living do you?'

'No. I pretended I'd never seen him before in my life, but I know Rachel's brother in law. Actually he asked me to have lunch with him—I wasn't going to, but now if he rings me I'll go and find out all I can.'

Sure enough Robin rang Kathleen at work the next day, and she arranged for him to pick her up at 1 o'clock. He took her to a small French restaurant, and as they sat waiting for their food he asked how the business was going.

'So well it almost frightens me,' she laughed. 'The premises next door are coming vacant, and I'm thinking of taking it over and have a little tea room where the clients can sit and watch the models. Just about eight or nine tables at the side. It will give the models more space, but it's only a thought at the moment.'

He shook his head in wonder. 'Kathleen is there no end to your ambitions?'

'No,' she answered, 'I seem to spread myself, but I think it would work.' Then quickly, 'But enough about me—who is the handsome hunk that Rachel is engaged to? What's his business?'

'He's a business consultant, has an office in the city and a posh apartment in Chelsea.'

'Well he sounds like a good match. Rachel is a beautiful girl—how long has she known him?'

'I think they met over a year ago. Old Ted wasn't very happy about it at first, but he seems to have got used to it now.'

Kathleen called in to see David Langham on the way home.

'I didn't get much on Charles,' she said. 'He's set up office in the city as a business consultant and has a posh apartment in Chelsea. I expect it's rented, but how is he making his money?'

'Well, when I rang inspector Duffy the other night I told him what you had told me, so he sent me a couple of plain-clothes officers in an unmarked car. They watched him after he took Rachel home and followed him to a rather run-down house in Battersea. Then a few minutes later he came out and they followed him to Chelsea. They're not sure, but they think he might have young boys in there working like Patrick. Anyway they're watching both places, and I'll let you know what happens.'

'God, he's such a bastard!' Kathleen was almost crying. 'I hope they get him soon.'

David smiled. 'So do I, but remember you won't be doing that wedding'

'That's a very small sacrifice for me to make. I would pay a lot more than that to get him locked up in prison.'

A week later David rang her.

'They've got him, Kathleen. He had two teenage boys in Battersea and he was sending all his queer friends there. The police caught two men when they forced the door. The boys said Mr Charles paid the rent and gave them pocket money. Charles turned up and was about to run when he found the door had been broken, but they got him. He's in deep trouble.'

Robin Delany called into Kathleen's boutique and told her the wedding was off.

Looking innocent Kathleen asked, 'Why is that, have they had a quarrel?'

'I think it's a bit more than that. Ted has told her that she mustn't see him or talk to him on the phone—she's very cut up.'

'Then it's as well it happened before the wedding. It's a terrible thing if he's not all he appears to be. There are a lot of con men about.'

Next day, Kathleen's secretary opened the door.

'Sir Edward Armstrong is in the outer office—he would like to see you.'

Kathleen was stunned, but said, 'Bring him in, and ask them to send up a tray of coffee.'

Sir Edward was ushered in; his enormous personality filling the little office.

'Miss Connolly, I am sorry to bother you. I won't take up much of you time.'

'Don't worry about my time.' Kathleen gave him a glowing smile. 'What can I do for you?'

'Do you know Charles Benn?'

'Yes I know him, and I know a lot about him.'

'Ah, perhaps you can explain then why Charles, when the police picked him up, said 'It's that bitch Kathleen Connolly, she's the one who tipped you off.''

'I think you had better sit down, Sir Edward. There is coffee coming up in a minute, and it's a long story.'

So Kathleen told him everything, right from Patsy coming to London with Gareth until Patsy's funeral, and she told him about her mother's trauma when she saw that Patsy was going to die. She also told him about Dennis and the IRA, and about Maura and Sean and Nuala and herself trying to get on with their lives, and how brave Rosie was.

Sir Edward listened gravely to everything she said.

'A brave family,' he said finally.

'What else can we do? We loved Dennis and Patsy and poor dad—now they're all lying together in a little churchyard in Ireland.'

'My son-in-law Robin Delaney, do you know him?'

Kathleen didn't speak for a minute, then she said slowly, 'Yes, several years ago we were sweethearts, but it went sour. I finished it, and that was that.'

'I think he still cares about you.'

'Well, it was well and truly over long before he met your daughter, and I don't date married men, and I would never go out or have an affair with Robin, I give you my word on that.'

'You are a good person Kathleen Connolly. I hope you always prosper.' Then, looking sharply at her, 'I hear you have your eye on the property next door. When you get it, let me know, and I will do your alterations free.'

'How did you know I wanted to extend?'

He smiled. 'Word gets around. Put your bid in. You will get it, I promise you.'

He shook hands warmly and left. What a good man, she thought. A good man to have on my side. I hope he believed me about Robin, when all the time what I wanted was his arms around me.

Chapter 20

Kathleen held the keys in her hand.

'At last,' she murmured to herself, 'I've got it, it's mine.'

She walked through the shop and out of the door and, fitting the key in the lock, she let herself into the shop next door. To anyone else it was rather a dismal sight—bare floorboards and stains on the walls where pictures had hung for years, now just white squares surrounded by grime. The ceiling was grimy too, with two long pieces of electric flex hanging down. It was a big room, almost square. She opened a door out the back—it had been the repair shop where the old antique dealer worked when he wasn't busy in the shop. A second door revealed a toilet and washbasins, rather the worse for wear. She came back and stood in the middle of the room stretching out her arms, and spun slowly round and round.

At this moment, the door opened and Sir Edward Armstrong walking in followed by another man.

'You got it then,' he said in a matter-of-fact tone.

'Did you not have something to do with it?' Kathleen asked.

'Not really, but I knew the people involved and I gave them a little push in your direction.' He turned to the second man. 'Kathleen, I'd like you to meet Danny Rafferty—he's an interior decorator, and great with colours and shapes. Danny, this is Miss Kathleen Connolly.'

Kathleen shook his hand and couldn't take her eyes off him—his Donegal tweed jacket was green, he had cream trousers and shirt, a green tie, the reddest hair she had ever seen, and he was covered in freckles—and she found herself looking into a pair of eyes as green as Ireland. When he smiled, his face lit up showing beautiful teeth.

'A tea room?' he said.

'Yes, a tea room—mainly for the customers, but for anyone really.'

He looked around. 'I'd like to open a way through to the shop—just an arch. Don't have a door if it's only for teas in the afternoon and morning coffee.'

'That's right,' she said, 'there won't be any cooking smell—just the coffee which will bring in the customers.'

'Good coffee I hope,' he grinned.

'Of course good coffee,' she snapped. 'There's nothing second-rate in my establishment is there Sir Ted?'

'No, Kathleen, nothing second-rate at all—and please call me Ted; I've never got used to the Sir.'

Danny was busy scribbling with a pen on a sheet of paper.

'I'm worried about the cost of it all.'

'We won't bankrupt you I promise,' Ted replied.

'There is so much to do,' air conditioning, coffee machines, and China, as well as furniture, carpets and curtains—and waitresses to find. Have I gone over my head?'

'I've told you, it will get done and it will pay for itself.' He patted her shoulder. 'Just leave it to Danny and me.'

Two weeks passed. Kathleen was wondering what the next move from Sir Ted would be, when late one afternoon Danny knocked and came in to her office. He laid a large drawing on her desk, and she looked at it, puzzled.

'Can you see your tea rooms?' he asked.

There was a dark blue carpet and powder blue wall, and twelve tables with pink tablecloths matched the pink curtains. The chairs had floral cushioned seats which matched the frilly aprons worn by the waitresses in dark blue dresses. The china teacups were patterned with pink roses, and an old fashioned dresser at the end was filled with plates and a flower arrangement.

When she spoke it was almost a whisper. 'That's exactly how I want it, how did you know?'

He grinned his cheeky grin. 'Well, it's obvious that we both have very good taste,' he replied.

He drew out another couple of drawings.

'You see there are two doors, one for the waitresses to come in and the other for taking out dirty china—it's a safety measure in case they clash in the doorway. The doors only open one way. The coffee machine is on this side and the dishwasher on the other side, and a glass fronted cabinet for the cakes in the middle.'

Smart pine cupboards lined the walls and there was a hot plate to warm the tea and coffeepots. Kathleen had to admit to herself that some of these details had never entered her head.

'There's an old hotel in Hampshire closing it's door for the last time,' he said. 'The auction is tomorrow. Would you like to come with me and bring your cheque book?'

He expected her to react, but she said simply, 'I would love to come, and I always carry my cheque book.'

'Great, I'll pick you up at your apartment at 8 o'clock.'

'You know where I live?'

'Sir Ted told me. And anyway, I know the district well enough as my father lived there sometimes when I was young.'

The doorbell went at 7.45 next morning. Kathleen was dressed and drinking her coffee.

'Sorry I'm a bit early,' Danny apologised. 'I was afraid I'd go back to sleep, so I've been up since six.'

'You live alone?'

'Yes, I've a bachelor pad—nothing special—not nearly as nice as this.'

'Coffee?' Kathleen nodded towards the coffee-pot,

'Yes please. I had a cup of the instant, but it didn't do the trick.'

She put a cup on the table. 'Help yourself, I'll finish dressing.'

Putting on her make-up she felt excited about her day ahead. Here was a very nice man—the first one to notice her since Robin, and in fact Robin's image was less clear now. She sang as she brushed her hair, feeling happier than she had done for years.

As they drove through the Surrey countryside, Kathleen asked 'Why did your father live near me sometimes? That's what you said.'

Danny laughed. 'He worked for the American Embassy. Our home is in Bray near Dublin. Father died ten years ago, mother still lives in Bray.'

'Have you served in the forces?'

'Yes, I graduated from Sandhurst when I was 29, but came out when father died. I didn't care for the life and only stayed there to please him. I did twelve years, and as I've always been interested in house planning and decoration, I did a crash course and then met Sir Ted. He's been a great help.'

'You never married?'

'No, I never seem to have the time—and until now I'd never met a girl I would want to spend my life with.'

There was quite a crowd round the hotel. Danny parked the Range Rover and they walked inside and picked up a catalogue. Kathleen scanned it.

'I'd like to look at these tea and coffee pots—plated silver it says—and this floral china might be worth a look too.'

Turning the page, Danny pointed to the furniture,' twelve small round tea tables with four chairs to each table. 'Let's have a look at those too.'

Kathleen was impressed. The furniture was in a good condition and the china was beautiful. And there were several other useful things as well.

When the auction started, Kathleen had made up her mind how far she would go, but the bidding was slow on the china and silver and she got them well below her limits. The furniture was brisker, with several dealers keeping the bidding going. Kathleen reached her limit, but to her surprise Danny took it up and got the lot.

'I didn't want to pay so much,' she protested.

He didn't seem bothered. 'If you don't want them, I'll keep them. They'll come in handy sometime.'

He arranged for them to be delivered and paid the bill, then he stacked the silver and china in the back of the Range Rover.

'We ought to stop somewhere for a spot of lunch. How do you feel about it?' he asked.

'That would be nice.' Kathleen was enjoying her day out.

Danny passed though some traffic lights and pulled into the car park of a large white building on the right. There were hanging baskets and window boxes ablaze with flowers.

'This looks lovely!' Kathleen exclaimed.

'The *Punch Bowl Inn* at Hindhead—one of the beauty spots of Surrey.'

They found the dinning room cool and very pleasant. Each drank a Perrier then ate a delicious meal followed by coffee afterwards. They risked their lives crossing the road to see the Punch Bowl. It was a lovely afternoon and the heather glowed pink, red, and white over the vast basin. Reluctantly they walked back to the car. Danny took her hand as they crossed the road, and he was still holding it as they reached the car park. And as he fastened his seatbelt he leaned over and kissed her cheek.

'I think I love you, Kathleen Connolly,' he said as he started the engine.

'You're quite loveable yourself, Danny Rafferty,' she retorted laughing.

'We had better put the stuff in my place,' Kathleen said as they got near to home.

'Yes the china might be safer there.'

'What are you going to do with all that furniture?'

'It will be alright at my place,' he said. 'I've got a big workshop. It's not damp, so it will be fine there until you need it.'

'We're going to have to talk money tomorrow,' Kathleen said.

'Okay, if that's the way you want it.'

Having put their purchases in the corner of the dining room, Kathleen suggested a drink—a cup of tea or coffee—but Danny just took her arms and kissed her gently on the lips, and she found herself kissing him back. Then pulling away she made for the kitchen.

'What will it be Danny, tea, coffee or alcohol?'

'A coffee would be nice,' he said.

She put on the percolator and hunted in the fridge till she found cream and a neat parcel of sandwiches.

'God bless Margaret,' she said. 'She doesn't think I eat all day. Sadly, today I can't do justice after that delicious lunch—what about you Danny, they look delicious.'

'I don't think I can, quite honestly. Put them in the fridge for another day.'

Kathleen fussed round the kitchen, getting out mugs, putting cream in the jug—always moving, not talking.

'Kathleen, will you sit down for a few minutes, you're making my head spin. Sit down, darling—we ought to talk.'

She sat opposite him and poured the coffee. 'So talk,' she said.

'I think we are deeply attracted to each other—are we going to ignore it? Or could we get a bit closer?'

'You mean have an affair, sleep together for a while till you get fed up—is that what you want?'

'No, it's not what I want. I'd love to sleep with you when you're ready, but please, darling Kathleen, don't push me away. Let me look after you—let me show you how I feel about you.'

Her eyes filled with tears. 'I'm afraid of getting involved—I don't want to get hurt again.'

He came round the table and held her in his arms. 'I've never hurt anyone in my life, and I'm not going to begin with you.' He wiped her eyes with a big white handkerchief. 'I want to ask you three questions—will you answer truthfully?'

'I'll try,' she whispered.

'Did you enjoy our day together?'

'Oh yes,' she sobbed.

'Do you like me holding you?'

A minute's silence, and then she said, 'Yes.'

'And do you think we can stay friends? Have a meal together, go to the theatre, all the things that best friends do?'

She looked up into his eyes, soft and gentle. 'Yes I'd like that.'

'Well then,' he said, 'no more mistrust. We will discuss and not argue.'

And with that, he kissed her forehead and left.

She sat looking at her mug of coffee, nearly cold, splashed it into the sink and poured another. She felt uplifted and happy. She hadn't thought of Robin Delaney all day, and she decided she wouldn't think of him again. He was part of the past, and the future looked rosy. Danny was such a lovely person, so easy to fall in love with. She would take each day as it came. Mam would like him, she thought, and his mother lives near Maura and Kevin—perhaps they know each other already.

Chapter 21

Kathleen spoke on the phone, to each one of her family. She wanted to tell them that Charles had been caught. He had been remanded in custody until his trial—he was such a slippery customer he would have slipped bail and disappeared otherwise. There was a long list of minor charges against him as well as the most serious one, the two boys for prostitution.

Rosie was glad he was out of harm's way. She wondered what had become of the boys—she prayed they wouldn't end up like Patsy. Kathleen assured her that the social service was looking after them.

Sean, Liz and Carol came to London for a weekend with Kathleen—things had improved between Sean and Liz and she was sleeping with him again, but there was very little warmth in Liz now. She felt the Connollys had let her down. She didn't understand the strength of the family unit—they helped each other under any circumstances, and Liz would have told the defender never to darken her door again and she would have meant it, but she was polite and helpful during the week end. Sean had brought his golf clubs and he and David disappeared on Saturday morning and Kathleen, Liz and Carol went shopping. They had lunch out and Kathleen showed Liz her big shop and the new tearooms.

'It's a pity Nuala can't run the tearooms,' Carol said.

Kathleen laughed, and said, 'Nuala would rather be a big fish in a small pond than a small fish in a big pond.'

Liz agreed. Nuala had a wonderful reputation in Cavan and she deserved it and she loved the country and the small town she lived in, and she was glad to be near mother since Patsy's death.

Liz looked at the outrageous creation in Kathleen's Boutique. 'Who on earth would wear that?' she asked, pointing to a white jersey silk sheath, split to the thigh and low V at the back nearly to the hips.

Carol said she would if it fitted her.

Kathleen wondered again at Liz, her Spartan mind couldn't conceive of anyone showing their naked back and one stretch of thigh. But Liz bought a shirt and top in very quiet colours, and Carol bought shorts and skimpy tops and a lot of underwear. Then they had lunch followed by coffee and an enormous ice cream confection, altogether a very pleasant day, and when the men came back, David stayed to dinner. Margaret had surpassed herself as each course was served.

'Isn't it a bit extravagant having paid help, for just one person?' said Liz.

'I would probably starve to death without Margaret. I don't have time to shop for groceries and I'd be too tired to bother cooking,' Kathleen replied. 'Margaret and I suit each other and I count myself lucky to have her, besides she keeps everything spotlessly clean and she does the washing and ironing, just like she did for Gareth and Patsy. She is a good friend as well. It's nice to come home and tell her about my day, and sometimes she and her husband have supper with me. I don't know what I'd do without her.'

When Sean, Liz and Carol left on Sunday afternoon, Kathleen sighed with relief. She loved seeing them, especially Sean and Carol, but she couldn't believe how Liz has become so like Barbara. She remembered thinking that Liz envied the young Connollys. She would spend the entire day with them when they lived at the cottage, and even after they moved she rode her bicycle into Belturbet every Saturday and usually stayed for tea, reluctant to go home in the evening. Now she criticised everything.

She asked Kathleen why she had a king sized bed, and was asked how a single bed would look in a massive bedroom. Kathleen had told her she hated the four-posters, so she sold it and replaced it with the king size. Was the four-poster an antique? Kathleen assured her that it was, and she got a very good price for it. Liz would have liked to ask how much, but Kathleen had left the room.

'Nosey cow,' she thought.

The truth was that Liz was jealous of Kathleen—in fact she was jealous of Nuala and Maura as well. They all specialised in their own field.

Maura was a head teacher and had a husband and two children and she ran her home very well, Nuala was famous for her culinary skills, and Kathleen lived with gentry and high class business people—and Liz had to admit that she herself amounted to nothing.

Just an ordinary housewife with very little skill and not many friends. Her son had left home, and in a couple of years Carol would do the same, and then she and Sean would be rattling around in a silent house. Sean had his work and a lot of friends at work; he played golf with them at the weekends and no doubt had a drink with them in the golf club afterwards.

Sean had tried time and time again to get Liz to play golf. He said it was great exerciser and a good way to make friends, but she wouldn't. She said she couldn't see the point in knocking a ball into a little hole in the ground. She would be bored stiff, and now she was at home twiddling her thumbs and everyone else was having a good time. Carol stayed in her room listening to tapes, or went swimming with her friends, or to the youth club or dreaming of the day she would move down to London with Kathleen. Liz knew if she went home to Ireland her mother would still keep on about her marrying a fenian, and what a mess she had made of her life.

Liz had another thing worrying her. She had a tiny lump in her left breast—she didn't know how long it had been there, just one day she was drying herself after a shower and there it was. That was three months ago. She kept touching it—it didn't seem to get any bigger, so she didn't do anything about it, but she thought about it often. She felt that she should have told Sean, but he would have had her into hospital before she could think, so she kept quiet and worried. He asked her on several occasions if she was all right and she assured him that she was—as right as rain, she said.

She wrote a long letter to her son Hugh, wanting to make sure he was still happy in Ireland compared to Manchester. It must be very quiet, what did he do in the evenings, at least they had electricity now and a television, but could he get a game of football or cricket? She was concerned about her father, Bob. Was he overdoing things? Another heart attack could be fatal.

She had a reply from Hugh. He said he was tired in the evenings, it was a bath and bed, he got up at 5.30 in the morning to get the milk out in time. Did she know that they had a milking machine now? The new milk parlour was great, so easy to keep clean. He was learning to drive and went to Clones with the Larkins to watch the match last Sunday.

Liz wondered what her mother thought of Hugh watching football on Sunday, but she knew that Hugh did whatever he wanted to do, and her parents had begun to rely on him.

He was all they had. Her brother Robert, after working in refugee camps for five years, had now settled in America and was married to a young America girl who was also a doctor. So there would be no help from him. All things considered Hugh could have done worse—a nice farm, and she knew there was plenty of money, and Bob cared deeply for Hugh. He reminded him of poor Hughie his grandfather—he had the same wide smile although he was taller than Hughie had been. It was a shame that Barbara couldn't forget that Hugh's father was a papist, but she looked after him well enough. Barbara was incapable of loving anyone.

Hugh hardly noticed Barbara at all; he lived in digs near college from Monday until Friday, then at the weekends he and Bob discussed the farm and what had to be done during the week. The Larkin boys worked well, and in a year's time Hugh would finish college and he had a lot of plans to put to his grandfather when the time was right. He visited his grandmother Rosie and he got a lot of love from her. Rosie was as broad-minded, as Barbara was narrow minded, and they cracked jokes together and he enjoyed every minute he spent with her.

Chapter 22

Liz Connolly dragged herself out of bed.

'What are you getting up so early for Liz? It's Sunday,' Sean said sleepily.

'I know,' she said. 'I want to go to church—I hope Carol will come with me.'

She stretched, and Sean grabbed her arm. 'What is that lump on your breast?' He was scared. 'How long has it been there, and why haven't you told me?

Liz stared crying. 'I thought it would go away,' she sniffed, 'I'll see the doctor this week.'

'You won't,' he shouted, 'I'm taking you to the hospital right now'

'No! No!' She was shivering. 'I'll go tomorrow.'

He took her in his arms. 'Liz, my darling girl, this is serious. Get dressed, don't have anything to eat, I'll be ready in a minute.'

He dressed and woke Carol. He told her he was taking Liz to hospital and he would ring later.

Liz helped the sister to take notes, and they decided to keep her in. The doctor would be round at ten o'clock and she told Sean to go home, she would ring him. Sean was reluctant to leave. Liz was very upset, but knew she was in good hands and Carol would be worried.

Back home, Sean headed for the kitchen. Carol was there.

'Cup of tea Dad?'

'Yes please darling—what a horrendous morning.'

'What wrong with Mam?'

He told her. 'She's had it for some time and she didn't say a word, can you understand that?'

'What are they doing for her?'

'She's seeing the doctor and they may decide to operate tomorrow, the sister seemed sure about that.'

'Will you ring Nana Barbara?'

'I suppose I had better.' Sean didn't often talk to his mother-in-law. 'I expect she will blame me for this.'

Carol put her arm around his shoulders. 'Don't worry about what she thinks—we all think you are a great dad and Nana Rosie thinks the sun shines out of you. Ring Nana as well, I'll ring Kathleen later.'

'We ought to go to the hospital this afternoon, your mother was very upset. We'll take some flowers, but it will take more than flowers to cheer her up.'

Sean was right about Barbara. 'Nothing like this would have happened if you had left her at home.'

Then young Hughie took the phone and listened to his father. 'Keep in touch Dad, and try not to worry. Granddad sends his love, and take care of Carol.'

Sean hung up the phone and put his head down and wept. 'Thank god for Hughie and Bob West.'

Rosie reacted differently. 'Would you like me to come over? I could do the washing and cooking and keep the place tidy.'

'That would be great Mam, but go and see Barbara, the dragon, maybe she wants to come and be near Liz.'

Rosie didn't want to go and see the Wests. Bob was all right, but Barbara never missed a chance to put the boot in. Anyone would think Sean was beating Liz everyday, she thought, instead of which she had been loved and looked after ever since she left home. However she got in her car and drove out—there was very little traffic on the quiet wintry road.

Barbara opened the door to her—not a smile of welcome.

Bob got out of his armchair stiffly. 'Nice to see you Rosie. Bad news about Liz—well we don't know until after the operation.'

'This should never had happened ...' Barbara started.

'For God's sake, Barbara be quiet. People get ill in Ireland as well as England. As Rosie says, it could be a benign—let's hope so.

'What I wanted to know is, do you want to go over Barbara?' said Rosie. 'With Carol at school and Sean at work, and going to see Liz, they will need a hand with the house.'

Barbara thought about it for a while and then said, 'You go over now and when Liz gets out I will look after her.'

Hughie came in and said, 'I think I will go over with Nana Rosie. I'd like to see Mam. I can visit in the afternoon and Dad can go over with Carol in the evenings. We can go together Nan.'

'Of course we can!' Rosie was touched at Hughie's concern for his family.

'The Larkins can manage. Now the harvest is in there's just the milking and stock—they've been doing it for years.'

Rosie and Hugh arrived in Manchester at mid-day on Tuesday. Sean met them at the airport and they went straight to the hospital. Sean had rung earlier and was told that Liz was comfortable, but she didn't look very comfortable when they reached the intensive care ward. She was very pale and she had a tube in her nose.

Sean disappeared to have a chat with the doctor.

Liz looked please to see Hugh He kissed her and sat holding her hand. Rosie was ill at ease. She kissed Liz and asked her how she was. Liz said she felt dreadful and Rosie said, 'it's early days and I hope you'll feel better tomorrow.'

She met Sean in the corridor. 'What did the doctor say?' Studying his face, she could tell without an answer that it was bad news. Liz was to start chemotherapy as soon as possible. They had to cut under her arm to the middle of her back. She had a 50/50 chance but a hard time ahead of her.

'Oh! Poor Liz,' Rosie said with genuine feeling. 'We must all love her and help her.'

The sister came up to them, and Sean introduced Rosie.

'She is lucky to have such a lovely family. Just what she needs for the next few months, but for now, go and give her a kiss and take that lovely son of yours home. Liz wants to sleep now. Come in later and bring both the children.'

Liz clung to Sean, tears in her eyes.

'You will be alright my darling. It's going to be hard, but we will all help you and your mother is coming over to look after you when you come home.' He kissed her tenderly; stroking her hair, almost in tears himself.

'I love you so much Sean,' she sobbed.

'And I love you Liz—we'll make it through this and be a happy family again.'

Rosie cooked a light meal for them all; Carol came home from school and was told the news.

Carol and Hugh went to the hospital that evening with their father. Liz had had a long sleep and she looked a little better. Carol was shocked—her mother looked very pale with a haunted look in her eyes, but she seemed more cheerful after her sleep. Sean talked gently to her and Hugh held her hand. After an hour she drifted off to sleep again and the nurse advised them to go home.

'She will be sleeping a lot and needs to get her strength back. Come in tomorrow,' she said bidding them all a goodnight.

Chapter 23

Three weeks later Liz came home from hospital, frail and pale. Sean carried her in and put her in the comfortable chair—even then she winced. Rosie had cleaned the house from top to bottom, and filled the fridge and freezer with cooked food which could be heated in minutes in the microwave.

When Liz was settled, Rosie left to spend a few days with Kathleen in London—she had an important piece of business about which she had told no one. The first surprise she got was when a handsome man accompanied Kathleen to the airport.

'Mam, this is Danny Rafferty.'

Rosie looked at him and smiled. Kathleen has found herself a real man here, she thought.

He stuck out his freckled hand. 'How are you Mrs Connolly?'

'I'm very well, Danny,' she answered as he clasped her hand.

Kathleen asked about Liz, and Rosie shook her head.

'She is so frail—it's going to be a long haul. Barbara arrived last night—she got a shock when she saw her. I believe the treatment is very severe, loss of hair and feeling nauseated. I hope it works. Sean is very stressed and Barbara won't make things easier for him. Hughie has gone back to Ireland—he didn't want Bob left on his own, he really loves his granddad.'

After lunch at the apartment, Kathleen asked, 'What do you plan to do tomorrow, Mam?'

'I want to go and see David Langham, your solicitor, and I hope to see your tea rooms.'

'I'll ring him for you now.'

Kathleen went to the phone, and when she came back she said, 'He's coming here tomorrow at 10.30.'

'How kind of him—I was happy to go to his office.'

Kathleen wondered what her mother wanted to see David for, but Rosie didn't volunteer any information and wisely Kathleen didn't ask.

David arrived promptly at 10.30. Margaret brought a tray of coffee.

'How can I help you Rosie?' David really liked this brave little woman. She must be sixty odd but she looked forty, about the same age as me he thought.

'This money of Patsy's which you have transferred to my bank, well I don't want it.'

David raised his eyebrows. 'What do you want to do with it?'

'I'd like the place where Patsy died to have it. The nursing was good, but the place looked shabby and needs a face lift and a steady income.'

'Are you sure about this, Rosie? It could help your other children.'

'No definitely not! They are all doing well without any help. I'm quite proud of them.'

'So you should be. I've only met Sean, but I hear Maura is a bright lady and I would love to sample Nuala's cooking and her husband's beer.'

Rosie laughed. 'You should go there for a holiday—there's golf and fishing and great walks.'

'Well, believe it or not I've considered just that. I've never been to Ireland, but I wasn't going for the fishing and golf—I wanted to see you.'

Rosie was startled. 'Why did you want to see me?'

'Rosie! Rosie! You are a beautiful women—I was attracted to you from the first time I saw you. I'm not trying to rush you—I would like to get to know you better. We are about the same age, I've lived alone since my mother died and you have since your children left home.' He paused. 'Do you like me Rosie?'

'Yes, I like you.'

'Well, can we go on from there, just a bit at a time please?'

'Alright David. I must admit I have been lonely at times, and I like your company.'

'Good, that's a start. So shall I take you out to lunch and a run in the country this afternoon, and perhaps dinner tonight?'

'Wait a minute! Kathleen will expect me home for dinner and I want to get to know Danny better. I think he and Kathleen are an item—they can't take their eyes off each other, or their hands.'

They had lunch and Rosie relaxed with a glass of white wine, then they started off eastwards. Rosie sat in the passenger seat, her hands clasps tightly in her lap. She had began to feel nervous again. David took his left hand off the steering wheel and placed it on top of her clenched fists. 'What are you frightened of, Rosie?'

'I'm not really frightened—it's just that I'm not used to being on my own with a man.'

'Dearest Rosie, I wouldn't harm a hair on your pretty head.'

'I know! I know! I'm just wondering what Kathleen will say. She thought I was going to discuss business with you for half an hour.'

'Well, we are going to Folkestone and back, and you will be home in plenty of time for dinner.'

'Thank you David, I really enjoy this attention.'

'What did you think of Danny Rafferty?' he asked.

'I was very impressed, he seems a caring person and he is very handsome—strong looking with lovely eyes.'

'He's all that,' David laughed. 'And great red hair.'

'I never thought I would see Kathleen falling for a redhead, but she seems deliriously happy.'

They wandered around and watched the ferries coming and going, sat in a little cafe and drank tea, then drove back to London. Outside the apartment he leaned over and kissed her on the lips. She kissed him back and then, blushing, she got out of the car. She didn't invite him in.

She wondered what Kathleen would think of her day out, but Kathleen was talking on the phone.

'Oh Mam, it's Sean, he would like a word.'

'Hello Sean, how are things?'

'Well, Liz is a bit low and Barbara doesn't help to cheer her up.'

'Where are you ringing from?'

'Oh I'm at work—it's easier to talk from here. I almost wish Barbara had stayed in Ireland, then I could have had someone cheerful in to look after Liz, but she is Liz's mother after all. If I keep out of the way, I'm neglecting Liz, and if I stay at home I get nagged non-stop.'

'Sean my dear, you will have to be firm with Barbara. It's your wife and your home. Don't let her take over. Have a word with the doctor, perhaps he will have a chat with Barbara.'

'Alright Mam. Don't worry yourself about it, she will soon get fed up and want to go home, and the sooner the better. Carol sends her love. I don't think she's very happy—when she wants to sit with Liz, Barbara sends her off, says she must not tire her mother. Liz loves to sit with Carol or me, but Barbara wants her to sleep all the time and then she can't sleep at night.'

'I wish there was something I could do,' Rosie said, 'but Barbara and me in the same kitchen doesn't bear thinking about.'

'I think perhaps the doctor would like her back in hospital. Carol said he said she needed a little exercise, and her legs are so weak the exercise would strengthen them—but Barbara won't let her walk a step. I must get off the line now Mam—I'll ring again tomorrow afternoon—take care of yourself.'

'And you my darling.' Rosie sighed as she hung the phone up.

Rosie walked into the lounge. Danny was watching the news but switched it off when Rosie came in.

'Oh please watch it if you want to, don't mind me.'

He smiled. 'I've seen all the main part.'

'What sort of day have you had?' Kathleen asked. 'I was beginning to worry, but Margaret said you had gone out with David, so I knew you would be alright.'

'He took me out for lunch and a drive down to the East Coast and we had tea and watched the ferries. I really enjoyed myself. I just wish Sean could be happier. What is happening about dinner?'

'Danny is taking us out.'

'Oh my, I'm really living it up—out for lunch, out for tea and now out for dinner.'

When they got back to the apartment after dinner, Danny said 'Goodnight' and left Kathleen and Rosie sitting together in the lounge.

'Are you and Danny making plans for the future, Kathleen?'

'Nothing definite, but I love him and I believe he loves me. We have slept together a few times, and that was satisfactory too.'

Rosie giggled. 'If you had told me that a couple of years ago I would have knocked you off your chair.'

'I know, but times have changed—I'm big girl now. I hope to settle down with Danny, but I won't rush him. What about you and David? I must have been blind—you are perfect for each other.'

'Hi, wait a minute! We have had lunch and tea—we are not planning to elope.'

'But you like him, Mam, and I think he kissed you—your face was very rosy when you came in—he did, didn't he?'

'Yes, he did, and I kissed him back—it was very enjoyable.'

'Well you old fraud, Mam—you have hooked yourself a great guy and you're blushing like a teenager.'

Rosie still hadn't told Kathleen what business it was that brought her to London, but at the end of the week she had a letter which she read and passed to Kathleen. It was from the secretary of the hostel in Redcar, thanking Rosie for the generous donation and the supporting income.

Kathleen looked questioningly at her.

'It's Patsy's money. I don't want it, and David has transferred it to Redcar. It will help someone.'

'What a great idea.' Kathleen nodded her approval. 'What else can you do with it?'

Chapter 24

Hugh, back at the farm in Ireland, was worried about his granddad. The poor old man looked very frail. Hugh hadn't seen him for nearly a month, and he had no-one to advise him. If only Granny Rosie was back—she would know what to do. Barbara hadn't mentioned coming home, and Hugh felt that Carol and Sean would be glad to get rid of her. Sean had plenty of money—he could afford to pay a nurse and would be glad to do so, but no nurse would tolerate Barbara.

He finally rang. Sean answered the call, and having asked how Liz was he asked to speak to Barbara.

'Gran, I'm worried about Granddad',

'What's wrong with him?' she asked.

'He is barely able to put one foot in front of the other—he's lost so much weight and he pecks at his food and eats hardly anything. I think you ought to come home—I've only got Mrs Larkin and she's nearly as feeble as granddad.'

'Alright, I will come home—I'll arrange it tonight. Sean will have to get a nurse in.'

'Thanks, Gran. I didn't know what else to do. How are you yourself?'

'I'm dead tired and can't think straight, and I will be glad to get back in my own bed.'

She rang from Dublin Airport next day. The Larkin boys went to pick her up. Hugh was reluctant to leave his grandfather, who hadn't got up that morning and was wandering a little as he talked. The doctor had been and left some tablets and just shook his head. Hugh hoped he would live until Barbara got home, but he was sleeping quietly now and they should be back from the Dublin within the next hour.

He sat quietly beside his grandfather's bed, heart broken watching the one person he loved more than anyone else in the whole world slip away. His shoulders ached and his eyes kept closing—he hadn't been to sleep for 48 hours. Finally he slept holding his grandfather's hand. He woke with a start as the door opened and Barbara stood looking at the bed. She seemed frightened, and he got up and led her to his chair.

She never took her eyes off Bob. She reached out and took his hands—he opened his eyes and smiled.

'Welcome home my love,' he whispered. 'How is our daughter?'

'She's going to get better—she's putting up a brave fight, as you must do. She will soon be over for a holiday.'

Bob shook his head wearily. 'I'm glad she's getting better,' he said again, and he quietly slipped away.

Mrs Larkin laid him out—the doctor came and signed the death Certificate, and offered to call in at the undertaker's and send them out so that arrangements for the funeral could go ahead.

Hugh rang Sean, Kathleen and Maura and went and saw the rector, then called in to see Nuala and Kevin.

'Poor Sean,' Nuala said. 'How is he going to tell Liz? This won't help her condition, and I don't see how he can come home for the funeral unless they take her back into hospital for a few days.' Then, looking at Hugh, 'This must be hard for you—you're barely twenty—your shoulders are too young for all this.'

Hugh squared his shoulders for her. 'I'll manage, Aunt Nuala. Granddad had been preparing me for this. I know what I have to do.'

'You're a fine young man—I'm proud of you.' Nuala leaned over and kissed his cheek.

Sean got home for the funeral after all. Liz was distraught, but she went into hospital for a few days. She wanted Sean to be at the funeral and Carol was staying with friends and would visit her each day. Rosie and Kathleen arrived home too—they had all loved and respected Bob West, remembering his great kindness years ago when Hughie drowned.

Barbara felt isolated—her daughter in hospital in England and her son in America. She wrote telling him of his father's death and Liz's illness.

There were so many Connollys, the church seemed to be full of them as well as all the friends and neighbours. Rosie and her girls got the food ready, and what a spread it was. Nuala had baked all the previous day and as usual the neighbours brought sandwiches and cakes and scones. Rosie's daughters managed everything discreetly and Barbara talked to all the visitors.

At last everyone had left. Rosie and Nuala washed up and tidied, and saying goodnight to Barbara went home.

'She didn't even say thanks,' Nuala remarked.

'We don't need thanks—we did what needed doing. Anyway, Sean and Hugh said thanks. Hugh was relieved when we took over—Barbara had no idea what to do.'

Sean got a late flight back to Manchester that evening—he wanted to get back to Liz, and hoped she was coping.

When he arrived at the hospital the nurse told him she had had to be tranquillised. She had been hysterical, crying and screaming, but was sleeping now.

He tiptoed into the little ward. Carol was sat beside her bed, and jumped up to hug her father.

'Oh dad! I'm so pleased to see you. Mam has been awful, I thought she would hurt herself. She kept saying, 'Let me die too, I want my dad! Let me go to my Dad!' Over and over again—I couldn't shut it out, and I couldn't leave.'

Sean held her close and stroked her hair.

'Hush my darling child, I did what I thought was best—I seem to be pulled every which way, but I'm home now to stay, to take care of you and your mother.'

Kathleen and Rosie sat with Nuala and Kevin in the hotel lounge.

'I hear you have got yourself a lovely fella,' said Nuala.

'Are you talking to me or Mam?' Kathleen asked.

'Don't tell me she has been husband-hunting as well!'

'Oh, neither of us were hunting. Danny Rafferty is putting my tea rooms together, and Mam got picked up by a lovely lawyer man.'

'Well, when am I going to meet these two lovely men?'

'David wants to sample your cooking and Kevin's beer—he might do a bit of fishing as well.' Rosie's face went red as Kathleen continued, 'Danny and I are coming home for Christmas—you'll meet him then.'

'What does he look like?' Nuala asked, and it was Kathleen's turn to blush.

'He's got the reddest hair you have ever saw and he is covered in freckles, and I love every inch of him.'

Nuala hugged Kathleen. 'I'm so pleased for you—and for you too Mam.'

'Oh, I'm not rushing into marriage just yet—I have to know him a bit better.'

'I've always hoped you would meet someone, Mam, but I couldn't see you finding a husband among the yokels around here.'

'Well you found one, Nuala—not that Kevin's a yokel.'

'Oh don't mind me,' said Kevin, pretending to be hurt. 'Yokel or not, I love you to bits.'

Nuala hugged him.

'Thank God for loving families,' Rosie thought.

Chapter 25

The telephone woke Sean at 6am. It was the hospital.

'Can you come in?'

'What's wrong, is Liz worse?'

'I'm afraid so, please hurry.'

Sean dressed quickly. He woke Carol to tell her, but she didn't want to come with him.

He met the sister at the door to the ward.

'What's happened?'

'She cried so much yesterday, when she woke up the mucus had settled on her chest—we think her lungs are affected.'

There she lay, propped up, her chest making a dreadful noise. Sean kissed her and sat beside her, but she didn't seem to know he was there. The sister stood at the bottom of the bed.

'Have you done everything?' Sean asked.

'Yes, but she is very weak. We have given her an injection to ease the congestion, but it hasn't worked and we dare not give her another just yet.'

'What are her chances?'

The sister shook her head. 'It's not your fault, Sean. Even if you hadn't gone to Ireland she would probably have gone hysterical at home and you and Carol couldn't have coped. We had a terrible time with her.'

Carol turned up at the hospital at 9am, and stood beside Sean.

'Why is she making the noise, Dad?'

'She has fluid on her lungs—she's very ill Carol.'

The doctor came round several times, but poor Liz got her wish and followed her dad. She died at Midday the day after her father's funeral.

Rosie and Kathleen came up to the hotel to say goodbye to Nuala and Kevin. They were having a drink in the bar when the phone rang. Kevin answered it and stood with the receiver in his hand.

'It's Sean—he says Liz has died.'

Rosie took the phone from him. 'Sean, it's Mam—what happened?'

'She got herself in a state about her father—the nurses couldn't control her, so they gave her something to make her sleep. When she woke up early this morning her chest was congested and she didn't respond to treatment. She died at 12 o clock. I'm flying her home to be buried next to her father tomorrow—could some of you go down to Hugh? Barbara has collapsed and the poor kid's at his wits end.'

'We will go down right away, son—I'm sorry about all this.'

'I know, Mam. I feel numb and so does Carol. It will be better when we're all together. See you tomorrow.'

'Bye son.'

Kathleen rang Danny and asked him to tell David.

'Shall I come over, darling?'

'If you want to—it's a sad occasion for you to meet the family, but I'd love to see you.'

Later there was a call from David. 'Danny and I are coming over—can Kevin and Nuala put us up?'

'I think so. Come anyhow, we need you.'

Liz's funeral was well supported. The choir sang her favourite hymns and the rector spoke very kindly of her and her family. Sean, Hugh and Carol sat together at the front of the church. Barbara was unable to go—she seemed to have lost her mind and Mrs Larkin was looking after her.

Nuala asked everyone back to the hotel after the funeral. There was food in abundance and drinks for all. Sean was grateful—it would have been impossible bring all the visitors back to the farm house. He was very lost—he had loved Liz since she was a toddler and he didn't dare to think of the future, their lovely home with just him and Carol. He didn't know how to bear it, and he knew something would have to be done about Barbara. Hugh had the farm to run and he wouldn't have a clue how to handle Barbara. He was surprised to see David Langham and Danny Rafferty, but they fitted in very well and he noticed David watching Rosie, catching her eye and the intimate smiles they exchanged.

Danny made himself useful, handing out food and drink and chatting with everyone. Sean liked him—he hoped that he and Kathleen would make a go of it. Danny sat talking to young Hugh, who cried off and on whatever he was saying. He nodded his head from time to time and blew his nose—poor lad, he had lost his Granddad and then his mother, not to mention coping with his half crazed grandmother, and was left to manage the farm. And he was just twenty.

Rosie walked down her garden path and sat on the old tree trunk under the hawthorn tree. She had a little while to herself for the first time in two days. Kathleen and Sean had gone to the farm to help Hugh, David and Danny had gone for a walk.

Dear David—he had been a tower of strength. She'd had a very depressed time on the evening of the funeral, sobbing. She'd said that every time she felt secure and settled, something awful happened. She'd been a contented housewife when Hughie drowned all those years ago—then having got her life together, found work and was supporting the family, Danny was killed—then Patsy's death, which still gave her nightmares—and now, just as David came into her life, the tragedy of Liz's death.

David held her in his arms and lent her his handkerchief to wipe her tears and blow her nose. The comforting warmth of him, the faint smell of his Cologne. She wanted him to stay there forever—with him she felt protected and safe.

'Marry me, Rosie,' he had whispered. 'I will take care of you.' and she had answered, 'Yes.'

Now she was committed and it felt good to belong to someone. She loved David, she knew that now. The blackbird still sang above her head—was it the same one or a son or grandson of the one that had sung there on the evening of Nuala's wedding, nine years ago?

They all sat down for dinner in the hotel. Nuala had arranged a magnificent meal. Sean, Hugh, David, Kevin and Ken, Rosie, Maura, Kathleen, Nuala and Carol. They ate and drank, and the conversation flowing until coffee.

Sean tapped his coffee spoon for silence.

'I would like to say thanks to you all for your support during this horrendous time. Thank God for close families, especially Nuala and Kevin. My concern just now is for Hugh. He is going to need help.

As you may be aware, Bob left the farm and everything to him. There seems to plenty of money, but he will need a house keeper.'

'I will come in every day until you find someone,' said Rosie, breathlessly. 'I will wait until they have settle down, but then—David and I are getting married.'

It had taken a lot of courage to announce it to the whole family, but it was done now, and they were all crowding around with kisses and congratulations.

Then Kathleen and Danny stood up holding hands, and Danny said, smiling, 'And Kathleen has promised to be my wife.'

More hugs and kisses, and as if by magic two bottles of champagne and glasses appeared. Healths were drunk and Sean hugged them all.

'I'm so happy for you Mam,' he said, 'and you and Danny, Kathleen. You are so right for each other. I hope you are as happy as Liz and I were.'

'Kathleen and I are going back with Ken and Maura,' said Danny happily. My mother lives in Bray and I want to show her my beautiful fiancée, and then we are going back to London where a lot of work awaits us.'

David said he would stay a few days.

'Can you put up with me?' he asked Nuala and Kevin.

'Of course—you're very welcome. What about you Sean?'

Sean looked at Hugh. 'Would you like me to stay for a few days?'

'Please dad. The doctor is taking granny Barbara to a nursing home, so it will be easier.'

'How is she, Hugh?' Rosie asked. She felt genuine concern for poor Barbara. 'It was enough to turn her head.'

'It did turn her head—she has no idea where she is or who she is. She called me Bob and she talks about Robert coming home from school, but she never mentions my mother. I'd like you to come with me and have a look at this nursing home. I want her well looked after. I don't know if she will ever be happy, but I'd like her to be comfortable.'

Sean went with Hugh and decided on a nursing home which was, light, airy and very comfortable. Nuala asked around for a housekeeper, and one day a woman came into Kevin's bar and asked to see her.

'My name is Mary Cassidy, and I heard your nephew needed a house keeper. I've lived in Dublin for 20 years, but my husband died two months ago and my brother persuaded me to sell and come and live with him and his wife. I didn't know my sister-in-law and I'm afraid we don't get on. I'm a good cook and I have always kept a neat home. I would be willing to help out with harvesting or whatever. I've never had children, although I would have liked one or two, so I've got no ties. My brother is my only relative.'

Nuala had a good feeling about Mary—she was quite smartly dressed and very clean-looking, fresh complexioned with well-cut dark hair, though her hands were working hands.

'Have you any references?'

'Yes, I worked as a cook in the Medway hotel for seven years. I had to give up when my husband became ill—they gave me a reference and I've got a letter from the parish priest in Dublin. He wrote it and sealed it—he said I might need it.'

'Why didn't you get on with you sister-in-law?'

'We haven't quarrelled, but it is becoming painfully evident that they are after my money. I have always saved, and I've got the price of my house in the bank. When they mentioned building an extension I said it was a good idea, and then they said they had given me a home, so I should pay for it. I have given them most of my widows pension and I've been doing my share of work around the farm, but I think if I paid for the extension there would be something else next year. Anyway, I told them 'no' I wouldn't be paying for the extension, and when I was getting my pension at the post office the postmistress told me about young Hugh needing a house keeper, so here I am.'

'If you could wait a few minutes, I've got a few things to see to in the kitchen, then I'll take you down the farm. My brother Sean is there with Hugh. You can see the house and they can take a look at you.'

Twenty minutes later they drove into the farmyard.

Sean and Hugh thought Mary Cassidy was sent from Heaven. She was just right for the job. The letter from the priest clinched it. He said Mary was a decent, honest women, a good housekeeper and was always cheerful. She had attended Mass in his church for 20 years and he would miss her.

She could start work as soon as she liked and as it was Friday, they agreed for her to start on Sunday evening.

Rosie looked in to see her the middle of the week and found Mary well settled. Laughing, she said she had found out Hugh's favourite food—the Larkin boys had told her—so the way to his heart was through his stomach.

Everything was clean and tidy and Mary had gathered the crab apples and was making jelly. After tea and fresh scones Rosie went home contented.

Sean and Carol returned to Manchester. Rosie asked them how they would manage.

'Oh we'll be okay,' Sean said. 'I can get a main meal at the canteen at work and Carol can get hers at college. I'll find someone to clean and do the ironing—we'll be all right. I might sell the house—it's too big for us. If I can get a bungalow it would be ideal.'

So everything was sorted—what seemed impossible last week was smoothed out, and Rosie could turn her mind to her wedding.

Chapter 26

Rosie and David walked up to the parochial house. The housekeeper left them in the study, and soon the new young priest joined them. Father Brian Martin was a pleasant change from old Father Brady who had preached fire and brimstone and put the fear of God into his parishioners. The young man smiled as he shook hands with them both.

'Mrs Connolly, this is a pleasure—it's always good to see you.'

Rosie blushed and said, 'This is David Langham. We would like you to marry us.'

'Does this mean I'm losing one of my best parishioners?'

'I'm afraid so,' David said, 'but we will be here quite often. Nuala, Kevin and the children are quite dear to us both.'

'Are you catholic, Mr Langham?'

'Yes, I was christened and confirmed in a Catholic Church, but I don't attend mass very often these days. But I am sure Rosie will see to it that I attend more regularly.'

'So when would you like the wedding? Two months or sooner?'

'Two months would be fine. I'll have to give up the cottage and sell the contents, unless someone wants to rent it with the contents as well.'

Rosie and David visited the family in turn and then booked their flight to London.

Kathleen, in the meantime, had found work piling up, and her constant absence was frustrating her senior staff. She rushed around smoothing ruffled feathers and finally everything had settled down. She arrived home totally exhausted, her head buzzing and her back and feet aching. Sitting down with a good cup of coffee, she lay back and closed her eyes.

She must give Danny a ring—she had only seen him once in three days. I'll ring him in a minute she thought, and then her doorbell rang and made her jump. That will be him she thought as she padded barefoot to the door.

But it was Harry Jackson.

'Kathleen, where have you been?' he cried, as he came in and shut the door.

'I've been to Ireland. Sean's wife died, and we all attended the funeral.'

'Why didn't you tell me—I've been worried sick.'

'I'm sorry Harry, I've been so busy. I've been home for three days, but I've been going early and coming home late—and I've got engaged.'

'You've what!' he shouted.

'I've got engaged to Danny Rafferty. He is an interior decorator, doing my tearooms.'

Harry grabbed her arms and shook her. 'How dare you! You can't marry him—you know I love you. You knew that, and you gave yourself to that painter!'

'Harry you are hurting my arms. I didn't know you felt like that. I love Danny—now please will you go.'

'I'll never go, I will have you, you two-timing bitch.'

He slapped her hard and she fell on the carpet, but he grabbed her hair and pulled her up and slapped her again. She fell and lay still.

Just then the front door opened and Danny came in. Wildly, Harry dashed out past him. Danny went to Kathleen, lifted her tenderly and laid her on the bed. He rang the police and the doctor. He had no idea who Harry was. Kathleen had mentioned early in their relationship that she sometimes went out with a Harry Jackson, but Danny had never met him.

When Kathleen came round, she cried and sobbed and finally was able to tell the police who Harry was and where he lived. The doctor said she would have bruises and probably a black eye, but nothing was broken—but if Danny hadn't arrived things might have been different. He left a few tablets and Danny said he would stay the night.

They lay in each other's arms and talked, and finally Kathleen slept. Danny lay awake and shuddered when he thought how it might have been if he had arrived half an hour later.

In the morning, Kathleen's face was black and blue. She wandered into the kitchen where Danny had put on the percolator.

'Will I ever look normal again?' she asked, tears streaming down her face. 'I can't go into work and there will be an uproar if I'm not there.'

'Don't worry darling. How about if I ring Ilish and ask her to come? She might take over for a few days. We will tell them you had an accident, fell down the stairs perhaps.'

'We will tell Ilish the truth, but she won't tell anyone—it would cause talk and be bad for business. I might be accused of bringing men home.'

Danny agreed. 'What about the police? Will they bring charges? They're coming round this morning.'

'I will drop the charges if he goes for counselling or treatment. I've never encouraged him, Danny. We were casual friends, he never laid a finger on me until last night and I've never wanted him to. Just a neighbour, that's all he ever was.'

Rosie and David arrived in the afternoon. Rosie was horrified when she saw Kathleen.

'I can't believe it, he was always so polite—not exactly charming, but always very correct.'

Kathleen sighed, 'I was completely fooled, I can tell you, but he has agreed to attend a psychiatric hospital so I'm not pressing charges—it would be bad for publicity and bad for my business.'

As the days passed, Kathleen's face faded and she went back to work wearing dark glasses. Ilish had everything in hand and Rosie's wedding suit was ready for the first fitting.

'When are you and Danny getting married?' Rosie asked as they sat sipping their hot chocolate before bed.

'We haven't discussed a date—next year some time, I expect.'

'Will you get married in Ireland or over here?'

'I'd like to get married in Ireland. Maura and Nuala did, and you are soon. It would be nice.'

'What's Danny's mother like? You met her didn't you?'

Kathleen laughed. 'You would never believe it—she is unreal. She obviously had red hair like Danny, but it is touched up, cut very nicely, and she is very tall and slim, smokes with a long cigarette holder and seems to always have a glass in her hand. She was pleased to see us, kissed me about ten times, said Danny had wasted his life, and hoped I'd keep him in order. We only stayed a couple of hours and she seemed relieved when we left. Danny was very quiet on the plane. I asked him what was up, but he said his mother always had that affect on him—she is so impersonal, we could have been any casual friends. I expected her to be pleased to see Danny, but she hardly spoke to him, just chatted to me.'

'Was he sent to boarding school when he was young?'

'Yes—he was sent away when he was seven, and he spent a lot of his holidays with relatives as his parents were abroad.'

'So he never really bonded with his parents—it's so sad. No wonder he loves you, Kathleen. You are so warm and loving, he must think all his Christmases have come at once.'

'Well, there was no lack of bonding in our family. We were always hugging you and crying on your bosom when things went wrong. It was lovely coming home from school, and you always ready to hear about our days—it's something I will never forget.'

'Sure, what else could I do? With wonderful children like you were, I was proud as punch of each and every one of you.'

Chapter 27

On a sunny autumn day, Rosie married David Langham. Maura was matron of honour and David's partner in business, John Knight, was best man. There were 40 guests, and the nuns decorated the church beautifully with flowers. The reception was at the hotel where they sat down to a four-course lunch. Sean and Carol stayed at the farm with Hugh and Mary Cassidy. Kathleen noticed Sean and Mary talking together, and Mary looked flushed and happy. Carol and Hugh, glad to be together again, sat side by side and chatted.

The photographer was busy and the grandchildren wanted to be in every group. At last Hugh brought the car to the door and Rosie and David kissed goodbye and were driven to Dublin for the flight to London. Next morning they were going on a Caribbean cruise. Rosie had never been further than London and was very excited.

Kathleen and Danny returned to London and tried to catch on their work. The tearooms were up and running and a nice women, a widow of thirty-five, was in charge and very capable. The little home bakery was delighted with the extra custom, and the cakes and sandwiches arrived daily, fresh and mouth-watering. Kathleen's clientele were pleased with the new service and the afternoon was very busy. She had a fashion show once a month on the first Wednesday, and it got so crowded that she had to have one on the third Wednesday too—business was booming.

Danny sometimes came to watch, and even offered advice about certain gowns. At first Kathleen was indignant, but found that he was often right—he had a good eye for style, it seemed.

Postcards arrived from faraway places. Rosie and David were having a wonderful honeymoon; happiness leapt out of every written word. Carol came down from Manchester—she seemed subdued. Kathleen asked her if everything was alright, and she said it was.

Sean rang Kathleen at work. 'Is Carol with you?' he said.

'Of course she is—didn't she tell you she was coming?'

'No, she left a note saying she wanted some time to herself. I've been worried; I don't really know any of her friends or what they get up to. She is very quiet. I know it's a few months since Liz died, but maybe it's taking longer than we thought.'

Sitting together with Carol one evening, Kathleen asked, 'Do you hear from your brother? I often wonder how he is managing the farm.'

'Yes he writes sometimes, but Dad and Mary Cassidy write to each other every week. He keeps all her letters in the drawer.'

'You don't read them do you?'

Carol blushed. 'I'm afraid I did. One day he was golfing, and I sat on my bed and read them all.'

'And that's what upset you.'

'Well yes—he seems to have forgotten Mam.'

'That's utter rubbish, Carol. He will never forgot Liz—they were childhood sweethearts, but she's gone and he is still a young man and he likes to hear how Hugh is doing. Mary is a nice woman. He would never take her away from Hugh. Maybe if Hugh marries, then they could get together—and don't forget you will be getting married one of these days. Try not to be selfish darling. Nan Rosie has found happiness late in life. We all find our niche. Now ring your Dad, tell him you are alright and will be home soon, and tell him you love him.'

Carol hesitated. 'I was going to ask you if I could stay—could I go to work in the salon?'

Kathleen didn't know what to say. 'I will have to think about it Carol. I can't answer until I've talked to your father and seen your exam results.'

Carol's presence in the apartment put a strain on Kathleen and Danny. She was always there. Gone were the times when at the weekends Danny stayed over and they made love whenever the mood took them. When Danny suggested spending time at his place, Kathleen wouldn't leave Carol alone in the apartment.

At last Danny rang Sean and suggested he came down.

'Is there anything wrong?' Sean asked.

'Nothing desperate,' Danny replied, 'but Kathleen and I can't have a life of our own. Maybe we are being selfish, but we are starting to squabble and we've had a great relationship until now. We hardly have a minute together anymore.'

Sean sighed. 'Believe me, I have tried to find a solution to Carol and her moods. I'll come to London on Friday evening and sort it out.'

They sat around the dining room table, Sean, Kathleen, Danny and Carol.

'I'm happy as I am,' Carol declared.

'You may be, but not everyone is,' her father said.

Kathleen put her hand up to Carol. 'Every single person in my establishment is qualified, the young ones have certificates and the older people have years of experience, so if you want to work for me you'll have to go to college and get good marks. I've been making enquires and you can get into Highbury Tech and there is student accommodation—what do you think?'

'I'm fed up with studying,' Carol mumbled.

'If you're fed up, then you can't be interested and you wouldn't be any use to me. All my staff are enthusiastic.'

'Well,' Sean said firmly, 'it's either that or you come home with me.'

Carol rushed from the room in tears.

'I'm at my wits end,' Sean said.

'She's had a rough time,' Danny put in. 'Rosie has gone off with David, and Kathleen wants to spend time with me, and she thinks that you, Sean, and Mary Cassidy are more than friends.'

Sean blushed furiously. 'Where did she get that idea from?'

'She told me you and Mary write to each other regularly.'

'So everyone is getting paired off, in her mind anyway, and she's got no one.'

Danny smiled. 'I remember feeling the same way when I was her age.'

'What did you do? 'Kathleen asked.

'I joined the army.'

'I don't think Carol would do that.'

'Give her time to think about college. I think she'll come round to it.'

On cue, Carol came back into the room and sat down. 'I'll go to college,' she said.

Sean came round and kissed her. 'Good girl!'

'Right,' Kathleen said. 'I'll take you there on Monday and I will take a look at the accommodation with you. You'll have plenty of friends—they are a friendly gang, and very casual—you'll love it, I promise.'

During the following week, Carol was accepted and settled in, and Kathleen and Danny had the apartment to themselves.

'I got the feeling Carol didn't want to go to college,' Danny said as he sliced the onions to go on the steak.

Kathleen, tossing the salad, was silent for a minute. 'Yes, I think it was the lesser of two evils. I wonder why she won't go back to Manchester?'

'I wondered that as well. It's not as if Mary Cassidy was on the door step. She must have got Sean's attention most of the time, unless he was playing golf in his spare time—just doing what he's always done, except that Liz was there for Carol in the past. Now she's on her own.'

'She always seemed to have plenty of friends and a fairly active life. Perhaps she'll tell me what's bothering her. I really love her,' Kathleen said, 'she's my favourite niece. I can see a lot of myself in her now she's eighteen. I wish Mamma and David were here. I don't know when they're coming back—it's been over two months since the wedding—it's a very long honeymoon.'

'David can please himself,' Danny said. 'He's a very wealthy man—he has two partners and it wouldn't surprise me if he decided to retire.'

Chapter 28

Carol was enjoying college more than she cared to admit. The two girls she shared with were jolly and very friendly, and a little lad called Robbie had taken to walking her home.

Diane and Flick told her to be careful.

'Of what?' she asked.

'Robbie messes with drugs and has some weird friends.'

'I haven't met any of his friends, and he seems fun.'

'Well,' Diane said, 'just be careful—it's easy to get roped in.'

On Saturday Robbie invited her to a party.

'What shall I wear?' she asked.

Robbie fell about laughing. 'Jeans and a tee-shirt, whatever.'

When he called for her they walked to a flat nearby. Loud music poured out of the windows—the place was crowded, couples sitting on the floor, lying in the corridors, on chairs. Someone brought them drinks. Carol sipped hers and wondered what it was—it was very nice so she drank it down and Robbie gave her another one. He was smoking and he passed the cigarette to her.

'Don't puff it,' he said, 'take it back.'

Her head was spinning—she felt light and floaty—they sat near the radiator, and he put one arm around her and the other on her breast. She didn't push him away; it was all so natural she drifted off to sleep.

Hours later she woke and looked around. People lay asleep everywhere. A man she had never seen before lay beside her, his hand on her thigh. She tried to sit but her head thumped and she felt sick. At last she got to her feet, swaying and stepping over bodies. She made it to the bathroom, but before she reached the toilet she almost stepped on someone—it was Robbie lying with a blonde girl, both asleep.

After throwing up she felt better. She looked at her watch—4.45am. My God, she thought, I've got to get back. She had a key, but could she get in without waking the girls?

She crept in without putting on the light, undressed and got into bed. She lay shivering. Who to tell and what to do? Why hadn't she listened to the girls when they warned her about Robbie?

At last she slept, and woke hours later to find Flick standing by her bed.

'Are you ok?'

Carol didn't answer but looked lost and pathetic.

'What happened to you?' Flick's arm came round her and she started to cry.

'I think I was raped,' she said.

'You think?—don't you know?'

'Well I drank a couple of drinks and I think there was something in them, and I had a couple of puffs of Robbie's cigarette and I think I passed out. I woke at 4.45 am, I was sick, then I came home, and that's it.

'That's not it,' Flick declared. 'Diane has gone to church—she will be home in a minute and we'll take you to hospital. Do you realise you could be pregnant or infected with H.I.V or AIDS or some other horrible disease?'

Carol started crying again. 'I wish I was dead,' she sobbed.

'You'll be alright—you're not the first to get caught in a drug scene, but just let it be a lesson to you.' Flick laughed. 'I sound like your mother.'

'My mother's dead,' Carol said sadly.

'Oh, I'm so sorry.' Flick hugged her again. 'Get dressed.'

Diane came in, and Flick took her into the sitting room while Carol put her clothes on.

'Poor kid.' Diane was soft hearted.

'Let's take her now—I'm glad I've got the car.'

Carol was kept in overnight and Diane picked her up the next day.

'They wanted to call the police,' Carol said, 'but I wasn't forced was I? However they say I'm OK. I wish I could forget it.'

'Well, when Robbie appears again send him packing. Come out with Flick and me—we have lots of friends.'

'Thank you, thank you both. I wouldn't have known what to do. I will be very careful in future I promise.'

She was pleased when they didn't say 'I told you so'. She made a vow to herself to work hard and pass her exams and make her family proud of her—but when Robbie raced up and held her arm, it took all the will power she could muster up to tell him to go away. Finally he got the message and left her alone.

Chapter 29

Rosie and David came home at last after their extended honeymoon.

They had left the cruise and flown to Singapore, and after a week there flew on to Australia. All in all they were away for nine weeks, and they looked sun-tanned and happy. There were presents for everyone—opal earrings for the girls and emerald tiepins and cuff-links for the boys, as well as toys for the young children and a lovely length of silk for Carol.

Rosie watched Carol's face as she undid the parcel—the beautiful silk of green shot with blue made her grasp.

'Nan Rosie, it's beautiful—but Aunt Kathleen will have to cut it for me, I'd be terrified of spoiling it.'

Kathleen watched smiling. 'Perhaps you could leave it for when a special occasion comes up.'

'Yes!' Carol said, 'I think you're right!' and she folded it tenderly and wrapped it up.

Now David had returned to work and Rosie sat sipping coffee in her big old-fashioned kitchen. The house had been bought by David's parents in the 30s and a lot of the furniture throughout the house had come from his grandparents and great grandparents.

Rosie had never had a grand home and she felt smothered by it all. The drawing room was a large room, but Rosie had difficulty walking through it, with so many tables laden with knick knacks, and a grand piano with at least 20 framed photos on top. The dining room had a long sideboard laden with silver and a big table which could place ten people, again a lot of pictures on the mantelpiece and a large open fire place. The study had wood-lined walls, rows of book shelves, a desk facing the window and two deep arm chairs, one each side of the fire place—Rosie liked this room the best.

A cloakroom led off the halls, and a grand staircase led to four bedrooms and two bathrooms.

Getting up and walking to the window, Rosie felt deflated. She wanted to run in the garden, but would have felt like a fool if she had.

Just then the kitchen door opened and Mrs North, the daily help, came in. Rosie liked her—she was cheerful and hardworking, and strangely she didn't resent Rosie at all.

'Morning Mrs Langham, there's a chilly wind out there this morning.'

'Have a cup of coffee before you start,' Rosie offered.

'A quick one then, I'll do the drawing room today—I dread it, so it's best to get it done. I only do it once a week now. I used to have to do it Monday, Wednesday and Friday when the old lady was alive, but now David hardly uses it.'

'I won't either,' Rosie said. 'In fact I've been thinking of packing away a lot of the ornaments. I can't stand clutter and it would make your job easier—in fact I think I will start today.'

Mrs North said nothing. She knew David had worshipped his mother—he might not like things moved.

However, Rosie found newspaper and a few large boxes, and started packing. Some of the things were beautiful, but she wrapped them carefully and three hours later, she felt she could sit down in the room. Mrs North thought it was a big improvement and hoped David would think so too.

Rosie cooked the evening meal, and when David came home he kissed her and she asked how his day was.

'Not too bad,' he said. 'I have a case in court tomorrow, I've been studying the papers.'

'What about you?'

'I've been working in the drawing room,' Rosie replied placidly.

'Doing what?' David thought the drawing room was perfect.

'I packed away a lot of the ornaments and moved a few things round—Mrs North helped me.'

David's face looked like thunder. 'Rosie, you could have mentioned it before you started—it's my house and I liked it the way it was.'

'You what!' Rosie exclaimed. 'You hardly ever go in there, it's my house now too and I'm here all day—besides everything is safely packed and wrapped.'

They finished the meal in silence. Rosie had no intention of giving in or putting everything back the way it was. Much as she loved David, she wouldn't allow him to tell her what to do or not to do. He would get used to the drawing room and Mrs North would have an easier time. Rosie could identify with her—she knew what hard work was all about.

Throughout the evening Rosie tried to make conversation, but a grunt or two was the only response from David.

At last, she put her needlework away and said she was going to bed. Another grunt from David was the reply.

She ran a bath and added a good dollop of fragrant bath oil and wondered what she needed to do to get things back to normal. She realised that if he had not mentioned how she had spent her day, it could have gone unnoticed for weeks, but she was very satisfied with her day's work and she thought the room looked charming.

Half an hour later as she sat at the dressing table brushing her hair, David came into the bedroom. He came up behind her and kissed her head.

'The drawing room looks great, Rosie. I'm sorry I am such an old bear!'

'I knew you would like it when you had seen it. We can use it now instead of the study. We will call the study your room—you can work undisturbed if you need to.'

The drawing room was indeed pleasant—most of the occasional tables were gone, the glass cabinet was still full of ornaments but a long low table near the patio doors held nothing but a huge flower arrangement and a few magazines, with an easy chair at each end. The long settee was around the stone fireplace, where another flower arrangement gave colour to the dull grey stone, and the entire room was fragrant with good polish and everything shone. That was how Rosie liked it.

Hugh Connolly stood in his barn, a deep frown on his handsome face. Things were not as well as he would have liked. The corn had been flattened by the heavy rain and thundershowers all summer, the milk yield was down and now one of his pedigree cows was lame.

Presently, a Land Rover swept up the lane, and was parked with some expertise in the hay shed. To Hugh's amazement a young girl got out, and with the door open she changed her shoes for a pair of Wellingtons. Well, thought Hugh, she can't be the vet—I sent for old Jamie Donaghue.

He walked down to meet her and thought how attractive she was—nearly as tall as he, black hair tied back with a blue ribbon, forget-me-not blue eyes with the longest black eyelashes, a wide mouth and even white teeth.

'Hello, I'm Pat Donaghue—I've come to see your cow.'

'I'm Hugh Connolly—I expected your father.'

'Oh him, he gets lazier by the day—he spends a lot of time fishing, but he does a bit in the garden and helps me out if I'm really busy. I don't begrudge him his retirement, he has worked hard all his life and he is seventy. So, where's the invalid?'

Hugh led her into the barn. 'It's her near front leg. I kept her in—I was afraid she would slip up in the wet yard.'

Pat put her gentle hands on the cow's shoulder and spoke softly to her. She lifted the hoof and rubbed her fingers over it, then she put it down.

'She's got a piece of flint stuck in there—I'll fetch my bag.'

Returning, she selected what looked like a pair of pliers.

'Could you hold her leg?' she asked Hugh.

He did, and she expertly pulled out a two-inch spike of flint followed by a mass of pus.

'Wow, that's nasty,' Hugh exclaimed.

Pat cleaned and dressed it and gave her a cortisone injection.

'Keep her in and I'll be back tomorrow.'

Hugh looked at the piece of flint. 'Poor old girl—must have been in agony.'

'Well, she's feeling better already.' Pat scratched the cow behind the ear. 'She is a lovely girl, what's her name?'

'Oh, she's Bluebell. They are have the names of flowers. My mother started it when she was little—now we're beginning to run out of flowers.'

'I didn't know your mother, but mother and Dad sent sympathy messages.'

Hugh nodded, then said briskly, 'Come in for a cup of coffee.'

Pat looked at her hands. 'I need a wash.'

'There's a basin in the office.'

Pat went back to the Land Rover, changed her Wellingtons for shoes and put on a neat tweed jacket.

Mary looked up and smiled when they came into the kitchen, and the large ginger cat jumped out of the armchair by the window.

'Pat, this is Mary Cassidy, my house keeper—Mary this is Pat Donaghue, the vet—Jamie has put the reins into her capable hands.

The women shook hands.

'What about Bluebell?' Mary asked. Hugh held out the piece of flint.

'Jesus, Mary and Joseph,' she exclaimed. 'The poor old beast— she must have been in agony. I suppose she'll have to stay in for a few days.'

'She will indeed,' Pat answered, 'but I will be out to have a look at her in the next day or two.'

Mary put two mugs of steaming hot coffee on the table and a plate of buttered scones.

'Oh those look good,' Pat said. She bent down to stroke the cat who had been rubbing against her legs, and Hugh noted with approval her very neat bottom. Mary saw the look, and thought this could be the one he has been waiting for.

Mary wasn't unhappy in her job, in fact she loved it—she did the house-keeping, cooked what she liked, went out when she liked, without having to ask anyone—but she knew in her heart it was only temporary. Hugh would meet and marry someone, and it could be this girl. Sean Connolly hadn't asked her to marry him yet, but she knew he would when the time was right, and she knew she would say 'yes' when he did.

Pat finished her coffee, having eaten three scones.

'Oh Mary, that was wonderful. It will last me all day.' She lifted the cat off her lap and stood up.

'Old marmalade has taken a shine to you—he doesn't make friends easily as a rule.'

'He's a lovely cat.'

'He is a spoiled old moggy—he fusses over his food, and Mary is always trying to find something he likes.' Hugh smiled at Mary.' But she does the same for me.'

'Then you're a lucky pair,' Pat said. 'No-one fusses over me.'

She said goodbye to Mary, and Hugh walked with her to her car.

'Thanks for everything,' he said. 'When will you be back?'

'Perhaps tomorrow afternoon.'

'That will be great.' They looked at each other, and both knew this was the start of a good relationship.

Pat hurried home, parking her car at the side of the house. She went through to the kitchen where her mother was just about to dish up the lunch.

'None for me, thanks mother.'

'What, no lunch? Are you in love or something? It's not like you turn down food.'

'Mam, I've just been to the Connollys, and I made a pig of myself eating scones and coffee.'

Her father looked up from his paper. 'How was the cow?'

'It was Bluebell. She had a lump of flint stuck in her hoof—I got it out and put an antiseptic dressing on and bandaged it, and gave her a shot of cortisone. I'm going back to see her tomorrow.'

'How's young Hugh coping?'

'Very well, I thought. He says it's been a bad year, he lost his corn and milk yield is down. I told him most of the farmers had the same story to tell. He has made a lot of improvements—the milking parlour is very up to date, and the kitchen is great, a lovely new Aga that heats the water and does the central heating—and that little scullery place off the kitchen is now the farm office. Mary says it makes life a lot easier with no dirty boots coming trailing through her clean kitchen.'

When Pat arrived next day, she found Hugh in a more cheerful mood. He hailed her with a wide smile—he would have liked to have hugged her. He had been thinking about her all night, and again this morning. He was afraid she would forget to come, but here she was, smiling at him, her blue eyes dancing. She really is a beautiful girl, he thought. He loved her capable brown hands with neatly cut nails, no long red talons for this lady, and her black hair in a neat bun on the top of her head.

'Well how is the invalid?'

'She's much better, I'm happy to say. She's had a feed of cow nuts, and she's chewing her cud and seems to have no pain at all.'

Chapter 30

Danny and Kathleen had a lazy Sunday morning in bed. They had had a late night out to dinner with friends, dancing afterwards and getting home late. Now they sat with a tray of tea between them.

'Let's get married,' Danny said, kissing her ear.

'Oh, I thought you would never ask,' Kathleen said, snuggling up to him.

'I've asked you every day since I met you, you tantalising female—so when is it going to be?'

'What about June? That's three months away.'

'Right madam, and don't you dare change your mind!'

Suddenly the doorbell rang loudly.

'Who could this be at this time on a Sunday?'

Danny struggled into his jeans. 'Well there's only one way to find out!'

Kathleen pulled on a tracksuit and ran a brush through her hair. Danny found two policemen on her doorstep.

'Is Miss Connolly in?'

'Yes she is. We had a late night—we've only just got up. Come in and Kathleen will be with you in a minute.'

Kathleen hurried in. 'Good morning, how can I help you?'

'We're sorry to trouble you at this hour, but your niece is in St James hospital'

'Has she had a accident?' Her voice was slightly shrill with anxiety.

'No, she was picked up unconscious besides a phone box. Someone had rung the police, but had disappeared by the time we got there. She had taken an overdose of some sort of drug—the doctors are working on her now. Can you come down to the hospital?'

'Danny, if I go with the police to the hospital, would you ring her father and my mother. I hate to do this to my mum, but she would never forgive me if I kept it from her.'

Kathleen hurried off with the police and was more shocked than angry when she looked down at Carol lying there, so white and still, with tubes up her nose.

'How is she?' The nurse didn't answer for a minute.

'We thought she was a goner, but I think she'll pull through—it was a very close thing though.'

Danny and Rosie tiptoed into the tiny ward.

'How is she?' Rosie s face was streaked with tears. 'I cannot believe this—how come we didn't notice anything different about her?'

The nurse smiled grimly. 'Junkies are very clever at covering their tracks. You would never believe how many parents ask themselves that very same question.'

Junkies! Rosie thought. She is referring to my granddaughter as a junkie—I don't believe it.

'She has been in before, not for drugs, but she had drugs in her blood.'

'What was she in for?' Rosie demanded.

'I believe it was a pregnancy test.'

Several hours later, Carol woke up to find her Nana Rosie, Aunt Kathleen and her father looking anxiously down at her. She looked so pale and ill—no-one had the heart to scold her, although Rosie was seeing her granddaughter in a new light.

Next day, Rosie and David took her home. She was quiet, and went to bed. Sean was at his wits end, and had no idea how to cope with the situation. He just sat on the edge of her bed, and held her hand.

'You're a terrible worry to us all. My mother has been crying all morning and David is cross with us all for making her cry. Do you think you can keep out of trouble in the future, so we can all live our lives in peace? I'm going back to Manchester now—if anything else happens I will take you back and put you in a clinic. I will not have you going the way Patsy went.' And with that, he bent over and kissed her. 'I really love you,' he said with tears in his eyes.

Carol lay and cried after he had gone. Next morning Rosie sat on the end of her bed and gave her the grilling of her life.

'Can you see where this lifestyle is leading? Will the college have you back? Do you know you're breaking your father's heart? He has had a lot of sadness, and instead of helping him you're a constant source of worry. So what's worrying you?'

Carol started crying again. 'Hugh has a girl friend now—he seems to be serious about her, and from what I hear she is definitely serious about him. Dad has Mary Cassidy all lined up—when Hugh gets married, Mary will be over to Manchester like a shot, so where do I call home?'

'So you take drugs and everything will come out alright? Even if Sean and Mary get married, it will always be your home, and don't forget Mary is a very kind person. She knows what loneliness is all about. You should be happy for them and happy with them. Now look at me Carol,' Rosie held Carol's hand tightly, 'and promise me you will fight this habit.'

'I promise to try,' Carol whispered.

'Who's Hugh's new girlfriend?' asked Rosie. 'I haven't heard about her.'

'You remember Jamie Donaghue the vet? This is his daughter, Pat. She's a vet now—she took over the practise when old Jamie retired. Hugh had to call her out to one of the cows, and she's been spending all her spare time with him since.'

'I remember her,' Rosie said. 'How did you hear about them?'

'I had a birthday card from Auntie Nuala. There was a letter in the card, and she says it's the romance of the year—everyone is talking about it. Mind you, I think Hugh is mad. She must be years older than him—she's about twenty six, I would think.'

'Don't forget how old Hugh is for his years—he had to grow up fast when he took over the farm—most young lads his age were playing football and chasing girls at seventeen. The poor love was getting up at five in the mornings, milking cows and running the farm almost single-handed.'

'Yes. I hope he marries her; it sounds like a good match to me.'

Rosie got up from the bed.

'Kathleen and Danny are coming round for dinner tonight. I think they have settled on a date for the wedding—that's what we are going to talk about. I am cooking a chicken stew, *cock-au-vin* the cookery books call it, but that's what it is with a drop of wine added. Get up when you feel like it—there's plenty of water if you'd like a bath or shower.

Rosie started work for the evening meal—consommé soup for starters, and lemon soufflé for pudding. There were a couple of bottles of wine in the fridge—if David wanted something different there was plenty in the cellar. Rosie still couldn't get used to a cellar full of wine.

Later sitting round the table Danny said, 'That was a magnificent meal, Rosie.' He smiled proudly at his wife.

'It was wonderful, darling—even Nuala would be impressed.'

Carol sat silently watching both couples. Would she ever have someone to tell her how wonderful she was?

David and Danny went down the garden and sat in the arbour smoking. Rosie went to make the coffee. Kathleen turned to Carol and smiled. 'We hope to have the wedding in June,' she said. 'I was planning to have you as my chief bridesmaid. Would you like that?'

'Who else are you having?'

'All your little cousins from Ireland.'

'I'd love that Auntie Kath.'

'You won't let me down, will you.'

Carol blushed. 'I'll try not to,' she said, hanging her head.

Kathleen put her arm around the weeping girl.

'Now tell me what that was all about? The nurse said you had a pregnancy test.'

'It was the first time, I went to a party with a young guy. I don't know what was in the drink, but it tasted nice so I had a coupe more. Then I passed out, and when I came round several hours later I made my way home. I had blood on my underwear. Flick and Diane shouted at me and dragged me to the hospital for an HIV test and a pregnancy test. Luckily I was clear on both counts, but I nearly died with embarrassment and I swore it would never happen again.'

Kathleen hugged her. 'You poor duck,' she said, 'you have really been through the mill haven't you, but you must put it all behind you now. It isn't the greatest sin in the world, but it could cloud your studies and I want you on my staff in two years time. I have been toying with the idea of opening another branch, in Birmingham or Manchester. I haven't talked to Danny about it yet, but he usually trusts my judgement.'

'Didn't you say once that you would like to get married in Ireland?' Rosie had been meaning to raise the subject with Kathleen for some time now.

'Yes that was the plan, but there are so many of my staff and so many of Danny's, that we decided to get married here and go to

Ireland for a blessing on the way to the States. We are going to visit Danny's aunt and uncle in Florida for a week, and then tour around for two weeks.'

'I would love to visit America,' Carol said wistfully.

'Oh, perhaps you will when you've finished at college.'

'I always wanted to go there, but I was turned sixty when I got there,' said Rosie. 'Have you given any thought to what the bridesmaid will wear?'

'I think a pale green for the little ones.'

'Could you make me a dress with that lovely silk that Nana Rosie brought back form Singapore?' said Carol. 'Would it clash with the others? It was just a thought.'

'It's a wonderful idea—and you would still be able to wear it for parties.'

Not the sort of parties I go to, Carol thought grimly.

Chapter 31

Carol Connolly was finding it hard to keep to the straight and narrow. Diane and Flick had finished college at the end if the summer—both of them had a degree in art and design, and were now having a holiday in Greece. Two young girls had moved in—they were younger than Carol, and she found them rather childish. Robbie had vanished, but she still went round with some of his friends.

She called in occasionally to see Rosie and David at weekends. They both thought that she looked pale and thin, but put it down to studying late at night and not eating properly—the truth was that she was still into drugs in a small way, she had many late nights and her diet consisted mostly of chocolate and crisps.

Kathleen's wedding was on a Saturday. The fashion house was closed at one o clock for the day, and all the staff were guests. The little bridesmaids and Carol all slept at Rosie's house and Nuala and Maura got them ready.

They all looked beautiful in their pale green taffeta dresses, and Carol was pale and slim in her lovely dress of Chinese silk.

Hugh and Mary came over from Ireland with Kevin and Nuala, and Sean drove down from Manchester on the Saturday morning.

Kathleen wore a cream silk dress with a lovely matching hat trimmed with roses. After a full mass, they all gathered in a big marquee on Sir Ted Armstrong's lawn—about two hundred people. There were gallons of champagne and a wonderful buffet.

At the end of the afternoon, a huge van came and took the wedding presents back to Kathleen's apartment—they filled her dining room and her spare bedroom.

Throughout the day, Sean watched Carol with anxious eyes. She wasn't right, but he didn't want to say the wrong thing to her. Everyone told her how beautiful she looked, but she just smiled and looked away—and when Mary Cassidy sat down beside her and tried to talk to her, she excused herself and walked off.

All the time Kathleen and Danny were away, Carol stayed away from Rosie and David's house. Her college work was going badly. The lecturers had more or less given up on her, and her head of department had written to Kathleen not realising she was on her honeymoon—and he just took it for granted that she had given up on her too.

The truth was that Carol spent very little time, and very few nights, at her flat. She missed lectures and did very little studying. She was into hard drugs—in fact anything she could get for her money—and when the money ran out, she had allowed herself to be picked up in cars. She didn't mind—just the money to feed her habit, that was all that mattered.

Kathleen and Danny came back looking marvellous. There was such a work load waiting for them both that it was several days before Kathleen got around to opening the letter from the college.

She rang her mother to find out when she had last seen Carol, and Rosie admitted that she hadn't seen her since the wedding. She said she was very difficult to talk to, and that she was sorry to say it was always a relief when she left. David had found her very hard work— she was sullen and bad tempered and seemed always to have a cold.

Kathleen went round to the flat, and the young girls answered the door. They told her Carol wasn't in, they hadn't seen her for a week and in fact she owed several weeks rent.

'Have you any idea where she might be?'

They both shook their heads.

'Could I have a look in her room?'

'If it's any help.'

They left her in Carol's room. The bed hadn't been made and there were a few items of clothing on the chair, but no worse than most teenagers' rooms Kathleen thought. She opened the drawer— just underwear and make up. Then she pulled out a pile of little polythene bags—all of them had a trace of white powder in them. She put them into her handbag. In the bottom drawer she found a needle—it was wrapped in her lovely silk dress. She put the needle into her bag too, wrapped in tissue.

'Where is it all going to end?' she wondered as she drove home.

Well, Sean would have to deal with it—she couldn't take any more of her crazy family's antics.

She rang Sean and then Rosie.

'I'm not surprised,' Rosie told her, 'but we can't have her here—David is not well. The doctor thinks he's had a slight stroke.'

'Why didn't you ring and tell us?' Kathleen asked.

'Don't you think you've got enough on your plate? I think it's up to Sean—he must see to her now.'

'Well he has to find her first,' Kathleen said sadly.

When Sean arrived, the look on his face said much for his frame of mind.

'What have you done to find her?'

'Well nothing really, I suppose. I've been to her flat, and the girls there say she hasn't been around for a week and she hasn't been paying her rent.'

She took the needle and the little white packets out of her bag, and laid them on the table.

'And I found these in her room.'

Sean looked at them in horror. 'Do you think she's dead?'

'Honestly, I don't know what to think—and to crown it all David has had a slight stroke, and Mam has to see to him and she is worried about Carol now as well, and she's not getting any younger.'

'I know, Kathleen, but she has always been there, and she looks so young it's easy to forget she is seventy next year.'

Sean went to the police station, and was shown into a small room with just a table and two chairs. A plain-clothed man came in and sat opposite him.

'My name is Detective Sergeant Hill—and your name sir?'

'I'm Sean Connolly. I've come to report a missing child.'

'How old is he, or she?'

'It's my daughter, and she is eighteen.'

'Ah well, you are reporting a missing adult then.'

'Yes, I suppose I am.'

Sean rubbed his tired eyes, and the interview continued. At the end, the Detective Sergeant said, 'You'd be surprised how many reports like this I get in a week.'

'What do you do about them?'

'We visit all the squats that we know, and we keep a look out on the streets—but she is of age, you do realise that. She is old enough now to do as she likes.'

Sean went back to Rosie and David's house, looking like a man twice his age—dark shadows under his eyes and lines around his mouth seemed to have appeared overnight.

He slumped in the chair and put his head in his hands. Rosie put a loving arm around his shoulders, not knowing what to say for the best to comfort him. At last he raised his head.

'I'll take a month's leave. I'll go up to Manchester in the morning and explain the situation to the board—they can appoint someone to stand in for me. Then I'll come back and comb the streets until I find her.'

'Do you think we ought to ring Hugh? I think he would like to be told.'

'Yes, that's a good idea. There's not much he can do from there, but she might get in touch with him. They were very close at one time.'

Hugh was distressed when Sean told him.

'I'll come over and search with you. Don't worry dad, between us we'll find her.'

Sean was getting very little sleep. He kept waking up then lying for hours imagining all the dreadful things that could be happening to Carol. When Hugh arrived two days later, both of them looked tired and drawn.

As they sat down with a street map and worked out a route for the search, David gave them some advice. They should work together, as a lone person either man or woman was very often attacked and robbed. Hugh's eyes grew round with horror.

'What, in daylight?'

'At any time of the day. It happens all the time, and some of the streets that you will be walking are full of junkies, prostitutes and pimps, not to mention car thieves and pickpockets.'

Day after weary day they trod the streets, the high-rise blocks and every sad little alleyway.

'Have you seen this girl?' Sean wondered how many times he had asked that question, but everybody had shaken their heads.

Sean's month's leave was almost gone, and Hugh had to get back to his farm. They had decided this was to be the last evening of their search.

They sat miserably in their car, trying to decide what to do, when there was a tap on the window. A women of uncertain age signed to them. Sean opened the window.

'We are not curb crawling if that is what you think.'

'I know. You are looking for a young girl, about eighteen, fair hair, blue eyes, about five foot three.'

Hugh's face lit up like a beacon. 'That sounds like my sister.'

'The next street to the left is Cotton Street. At the bottom end is No. 30. Take a policeman or two with you—there are several men in there and they are all dangerous.'

'Why are you telling us this? What's in it for you?'

'I earn my living on the streets, and it's a good living. Now these boys go and pick up our customers and take them back to No. 30.'

'Have you seen the girl?'

'Yes several times. There is another girl, a coloured girl. They don't get out much—they both look drugged.'

Sean took a fifty-pound out of his wallet and handed it to her.

She grinned,' 'Are you sure you don't want something for your money.'

He shook his head, and said softly, 'I just want my daughter back safely.'

The woman slipped away into the darkness. Hugh looked at his father.

'Where do we go from here?'

'To the police station, I think.'

At the police station, the sergeant he had talked to before called them both into a side room. They told him what the women had said.

'Do you know this person?'

'No—I believe her though. She said quite frankly that she was living on the streets.'

'Did she ask for your money?'

'No, but I gave her some.'

The policeman laughed. 'I think she saw you coming.'

Hugh spoke for the first time. 'Well, are you going to give her the benefit of the doubt?'

'I will have to talk to my superior.'

'How long will that take?'

'A couple of days.'

'As long as that? That's not good enough.'

Hugh stood up, and looked the policeman in the eye.

'My father has a business to run in Manchester and I have a farm in Ireland that needs my attention, so tomorrow morning at eight o'clock we will be calling at that house whether you are there or not.'

The policeman looked flustered.

'I hope you are not going to take the law into your own hands, because you could be in serious trouble.'

'We are not violent people, sir, we just want to talk to my sister.'

The sergeant didn't like these two—they were not afraid of him, that was obvious. He was a vain man, accustomed to dealing with criminals, but these two had nothing to hide.

'Do you think he will turn up tomorrow?' Hugh asked as they got back in the car.

'I think they will. Perhaps not him, but they will send someone along, just to make sure we don't get hurt.'

Just as Sean had predicted a police car was parked below the house as Sean and Hugh got out of the car. The two uniformed policemen got out of theirs.

Sean knocked smartly on the door, and it was opened by a young coloured man.

'Can I speak to Carol, please?' said Sean.

'I think she is still in bed, I'll give her a knock.'

They waited a few minutes—then Carol came down the stairs in a dressing gown, followed by a tall coloured man. She looked startled when she saw them.

'What are you two doing here?'

'I think the question is, what are you doing here. The last time I saw you, you were at college. I would like to know why you have given up your education, moved out of your flat and caused my mother and Kathleen sleepless nights wondering if you were dead or alive.'

Sean was angry. All the pent-up emotions of the last month were overflowing.

Hugh laid a hand on his fathers arm. 'Hush, Dad, let her speak.'

Sean looked with hard eyes at his daughter and her companion.

'Right, Carol, explain yourself.'

She hesitated, looked nervously at the man beside her, then said, 'Dad, I'm staying here with Jack. He looks after me very well. I am not going back home or back to college.'

'You don't look well to me,' said Hugh.

The man beside her smiled, and put his arm around her.

'You'll be alright presently, babe,' he said grinning defiantly at Sean and Hugh.

'Well then, there isn't much more to say.'

Sean turned on his heel and, followed by Hugh, left the building.

'What do you think he meant, she would be alright presently?'

One of the policeman spoke. 'He probably means a shot in the arm. I noticed the needle marks in her arm.'

Hugh stopped. 'I'm going back to drag her out of there.'

The two policeman closed around him.

'It's no good son,' Sean said wearily. 'she would only run away again. She will either wake up one day and drag herself out, or she will die on the streets.'

Rosie made them a cup of tea.

'I blame myself for all this nonsense.'

'Mother, how could you have prevented it. As the policeman pointed out, she is an adult, and I think she was well into drugs while she was at college.'

Next morning Sean set off for Manchester and Hugh went to the airport. Pat was at Dublin to meet him, and held him in her arms. They had talked every night on the phone, and she knew the pain he was suffering.

'I couldn't believe my eyes. This pathetic skinny girl leaning on a repulsive man, and him almost spelling it out that he had a fix for her. Look after her indeed!'

In Manchester, Sean was pouring out his soul to Mary Cassidy on the phone.

At the end of it he said, 'Come over here and marry me, Mary. I never thought I would love again after Liz, but Liz and I were children. We rushed into things, we knew very little about things and when she became pregnant I almost dragged her over to England to make an honest women of her. And to give us both credit, we stayed faithful to each other for the whole marriage, but there were times when I felt like running away. I think we both grew up and away from each other.'

Mary listened quietly, then said, 'Sean dear, of course I will marry you. As soon as Hugh and Pat get back from their honeymoon, I will come to you. Their wedding is next month and they are going to the States for three weeks. After that, I will be free. I must say that I've loved it here, and if you're as easy to live with as Hugh, I'll have nothing to worry about.'

Chapter 32

Hugh and Pat were married on the 23rd September. So that Nuala and Kevin could relax and enjoy the day, the reception was held at the Russell Hotel in the nearby town of Ballconnel. Nuala whispered that she was dying to see the inside of this magnificent hotel. A great fuss had been made at the opening a few years ago, but everyone agreed that the meal was no better than they would have got at Nuala's, and after much merrymaking the happy couple were driven to Dublin *en route* to New York.

Sean and Mary went back to the farm. The Larkin brothers were finishing the milking, one turning the cows out to the field and the other hosing the milking parlour and putting the milk in the cold room.

Sean remarked how different it all was since his day, working for Bob West with his father.

'It's a great improvement since we came here—I'm surprised neither of you ever got married.'

The two brothers laughed.

'Why should we bother,' said one.

'We pick and choose, even though we are nearly fifty,' said the other.

'Now is it true what they tell us?' said the first, 'that you and Mary are going to get hitched. Sure, it would be a great match entirely.'

Sean blushed scarlet. 'I have to admit we have talked about it, but nothing is settled yet.'

'Ah well, good luck to both of you.'

Chapter 33

The air was still warm from the summer sunshine, and bird song drifted through the open window as Rosie Langham sat quietly looking out at her garden. She hadn't fell in love with the house but with the garden. The grounds had been laid out by Capability Brown many years ago and had been maintained carefully ever since.

After David's death five years ago, she thought of selling, but her son-in-law pointed out that it wasn't the house she disliked but the massive Victorian furniture, so she sold a lot of the old stuff and replaced it with light modern furniture and found that Danny was right.

So here she was, the day before her 80th birthday, totally at peace with the world.

A great many of her family were coming later that day.

Her son Sean and his wife Mary were coming from Manchester, and Maura and Ken from Dublin, and Carol.

She thought back with horror on Carol's life, living with a coloured man and deeply into drugs—then Barbara West, Sean's mother-in-law had died, and the lawyer produced a will which she had made when Carol was only a baby—leaving Carol £5,000.

The family had groaned—she would buy a lot of drugs with £5,000. But she surprised them all, getting herself into a clinic and coming out six months later, to all intent and purpose cured. She went to live in a hostel to counsel drug addicts and, refusing all help from her family, she was now in charge of the daily running of the clinic.

Rosie had written with an invitation to her birthday party, and to everyone's surprise she had agreed to come.

Looking out through the kitchen window, she saw a large car pull up and another one follow.

Kathleen and Danny got out of the first and four people from the second. For a minute, Rosie couldn't think who they were—but then she saw that it was Sean, Mary, Ken and Maura.

She filled the kettle quickly and went to meet them—hugs and kisses all round.

'How did you four meet up?' she asked Sean.

Maura answered. 'We flew to Manchester. It was quicker and cheaper and we've all driven down together.'

They chatted over a cup of tea, and Rosie said, 'Sean, your daughter is coming tomorrow, to my party. I want you to make her feel welcome.'

'I haven't seen her in years, but I ring her and she rings me.'

At that moment Rosie's phone rang. Kathleen answered it, and an unfamiliar voice said, 'Can I speak to Mrs Rosie Langham, please.'

Rosie hurried to the phone.

'Hello Nan, it's Carol here. Can I bring a friend to your party tomorrow?'

'Of course you can, as many as you like. I am looking forward to seeing you darling. Your father is here—do you want a word with him?'

'No,' she said, 'I'll speak to them all tomorrow. Good bye Nan, God bless.'

'God bless to you darling.'

Rosie put the phone down. 'It was Carol. She's bringing a friend tomorrow.'

Then seeing their faces all registering dismay, she said firmly, 'Whoever it is or what it is, they are welcome in my house. I've waited a long time to get Carol back, and I have no intentions of losing her again. You can all think what you like, but don't let it show.'

At the party, they eagerly awaited Carol. She arrived looking smart in a grey trouser suit, her long hair in a fat chignon with a diamond clasp. She was accompanied by a tall well-dressed man in his fifties, and he held her hand as she introduced him to her family.

'This is John McKinsey Cooper,' she told them all proudly. 'He works with me at the rehab centre. John, this is my Nan, and this is my father. You will get the hang of them presently.'

Kevin and Nuala arrived late and flustered, blaming traffic on both sides of the water. Kevin had put on a lot of weight, Rosie noticed, but Nuala was as slim as a whippet.

Later John Mc Kinsey Cooper stood up.

'I am happy to be able to tell you that Carol and I were married this morning.'

There was a few seconds silence, then everyone was hugging Carol and shaking hands with John.

Sean clasped his hand. 'Welcome to the family,' he said. 'You will take care of her, I know.'

'Yes,' John said. 'I love here very much and I know what she has been through—she will be safe with me.'

Chapter 34

The old farm kitchen was quiet, just the ancient clock ticking away. A small girl bent over her homework as she wrote furiously. A burst of childish laughter sounded through the open window.

The clock stuck five as young Rose Connolly gathered up her books. She pushed them into her satchel and ran out of the door, black curls bobbing up and down, to join her young brothers in the hay field.

www.ingramcontent.com/pod-product-compliance
Lightning Source LLC
Chambersburg PA
CBHW051104050726